WAYSIDE SCHOOL
Gets a Little
STRANGER

WAYSIDE SCHOOL Gets a Little STRANGER

Louis Sachar
illustrated by Joel Schick

Morrow Junior Books
New York

Text copyright © 1995 by Louis Sachar
Illustrations copyright © 1995 by Joel Schick

09 10 11 12 13 CG/RRDB 20 19 18 17 16 15 14 13

Library of Congress Cataloging-in-Publication Data
Sachar, Louis.
Wayside School gets a little stranger/by Louis Sachar. p. cm.
Summary: Unusual things continue to happen in the classroom on the
thirtieth floor of Wayside School, which was accidentally built sideways
with one classroom on each story. ISBN 0-688-13694-X
[1. Schools—Fiction. 2. Humorous stories.] I. Title.
PZ7.S1185Wav 1995 [Fic]—dc20 94-25448 CIP AC

To Carla and Sherre, with love

Contents

1. Explanation

For two hundred and forty-three days, a lonely sign hung on the front of the old school building.

Wayside School
Closed for Repairs

On some days a child would come, look at the sign, then sadly walk away.

Or else a child would come, look at the sign, stand on her head, then sadly walk away.

Louis watched them come and go.

But he never said "Hi!" to them. He hid when they came.

It was his job to repair the school.

Louis used to be the yard teacher at Wayside School. He passed out the balls and played with the kids at recess and lunch.

When the school closed, the children were sent to other schools. Horrible schools. No two kids were sent to the same school.

Louis was afraid he'd cry if he talked to them.

But he worked hard. For two hundred and forty-two days, he pushed and pulled, shoveled and mopped. He never left the building. At night he slept on the couch in the teachers' lounge on the twelfth floor.

Some days it seemed hopeless. The worst part was the smell. He often had to run and stick his head out a window to get a breath of fresh air. But whenever he felt like quitting, he thought about those poor kids, stuck in those horrible schools, and he just worked harder.

And at last, two hundred and forty-three days later, the school was ready to open.

Well, almost ready. There was one little problem.

Suddenly, from somewhere inside the building, or maybe just inside his head, Louis heard a loud "moo."

He put his hands over his ears and said, "I don't hear it, I don't hear it, I don't hear it," until the mooing stopped.

He had scrubbed and polished every inch of Wayside School. There were no cows anywhere. He was sure of it! Still, every once in a while, he heard something go "moo." Or at least he thought he did.

He took the sign off the door.

But before you enter, you should know something about Wayside School.

Wayside School is a thirty-story building with one room on each floor, except there is no nineteenth story.

Mrs. Jewls teaches the class on the thirtieth story.

Miss Zarves teaches the class on the nineteenth story. There is no Miss Zarves.

Understand?

Good; explain it to me.

"Louis!" someone shouted.

He turned to see a red and blue overcoat

running toward him. "Hi, Sharie!" he said. He couldn't see her face, but he knew she had to be somewhere inside the coat.

Sharie jumped into his arms.

"I bet you're glad to be back," said Louis.

"You bet!" said Sharie. "Now I can finally get some sleep!"

All around the playground, old friends were getting back together.

"Hi, old pal!" said John.

"Hey, good buddy," said Joe.

"Bebe!" yelled Calvin from one side of the playground.

"Calvin!" shouted Bebe from the other.

They ran and smashed into each other.

"Hi, Eric, good to see you," said Eric.

"Hey, good to see you too," said Eric. "Oh, look. There's Eric!"

"Hi, Eric! Hi, Eric!"

"Hi, Eric."

"Hi, Eric."

Even Kathy said hello to everybody.

"Hey, Big Ears!" she said to Myron as she slapped him on the back. "What's happ'nin', Smelly?" she asked Dameon. "You didn't take a bath for two hundred and forty-three days, did you? Hi, Allison. Did you get uglier while you were

4

away, or were you always this ugly and I just forgot?"

"That's a nice sweater, Kathy," said Allison, who always tried to say something nice.

Kathy moved on to Terrence. "I'm sure glad to see you, Terrence!" she said.

"You are?" asked Terrence.

"Yes," said Kathy. "I thought you'd be in jail by now."

Todd came running across the playground.

"Hi, Todd!" shouted Sharie, right in Louis's ear.

Todd kept running.

"Hey, Todd!" called Jason. "Good to see you!"

"Hi, Todd!" called Myron and D.J.

But Todd didn't answer. He just kept running until he reached the school building.

Then he kissed Wayside School.

Out of all the schools, Todd had been sent to the very worst one. It was awful! The first thing he had to do every morning was—

Wait a second. I don't have to tell you. You already know.

Todd was sent to your school.

2. A Message from the Principal

Dameon hurried up the stairs. He couldn't wait to see Mrs. Jewls, his favorite teacher in the whole world.

But the thirtieth floor was a lot higher up than he remembered, even if there was no nineteenth.

By the time he got up there, his legs hurt, his side ached, and he had a blister on the back of his ankle where it rubbed against his sneaker.

He stumbled into the room and collapsed on the floor. "Hi, Mrs. Jewls," he gasped.

"Hi, Dameon, welcome back!" said Mrs. Jewls.

Dameon looked up at her. Something seemed different about her, but he wasn't sure what it was.

"Oh, Dameon, would you do me a favor?" she asked.

"Sure," said Dameon.

"I left my pencil in the office," said Mrs. Jewls. "Would you mind going down and getting it for me?"

"No problem," said Dameon.

"It's yellow," said Mrs. Jewls. "It has a point at one end and a red eraser at the other."

Dameon got to his feet and headed down the stairs.

One by one the other children staggered into the classroom, huffing and puffing. They were all out of shape.

Still, they were very excited to be back in Mrs. Jewls's class. Shouts of joy could be heard from every corner of the room.

Mrs. Jewls held up two fingers.

All the children became quiet. Joy stopped shouting.

Mrs. Jewls told the children to sit at their old desks. "So, did anyone learn anything at your other schools?" she asked.

Mac raised his hand. "Oooh! Oooh!" he grunted.

"Yes, Mac," said Mrs. Jewls.

"Civilization!" declared Mac.

"What about civilization?" asked Mrs. Jewls.

"We learned it," said Mac.

"That's very impressive," said Mrs. Jewls. "Would you like to tell the class something about civilization?"

Mac thought a moment. "I don't remember," he said. "But I know we learned it."

"That's good, Mac," said Mrs. Jewls. "Anyone else learn anything?"

Rondi raised her hand. "Evaporation," she said.

"Good," said Mrs. Jewls. "What is evaporation?"

"I don't know," said Rondi.

Dana raised her hand. "I learned about exaggeration," she said. "It was all my teacher ever talked about. We had like ten thousand tests on it, and the teacher would kill you if you didn't spell it right."

"That's very good, Dana!" said Mrs. Jewls. "You learned your lesson well."

"I did?" asked Dana.

Mrs. Jewls shrugged. "Well, I guess we'll just continue where we left off."

Just then Mr. Kidswatter's voice came over the P.A. system. **"Good morning, boys and girls."**

Mr. Kidswatter was the principal. He paused a moment because he thought every kid in school was saying "Good morning, Mr. Kidswatter" back to him.

Nobody said it.

Sharie buried her head in her huge coat, closed her eyes, and went to sleep.

"Welcome back to Wayside School!" said Mr. Kidswatter. **"I know I'm sure glad to be back. It was wonderful to see all your bright and chipper faces this morning. I missed every single one of you.**

"And welcome back to Miss Mush, too. Today's lunch menu will be baked liver in purple sauce. Miss Mush actually cooked this before the school was closed, but she assures me it is still as tasty as ever!"

"I'm sure it is," said Myron.

"A safety reminder. Now, it has been a while since you've had to rush up and down the stairs, and I want to make sure there are no accidents. So remember this simple rule. When you go up the stairs, stay to your right. When you go down the stairs, stay to your left. That way, there should be no problems.

"Okay, let's all have a good day. And re-

9

member, I'm your friend. And you're my friends. And if you ever need a friend, you can always come to me."

"Isn't that nice," said Mrs. Jewls.

"What a bunch of baloney! There I was, lying on a beach in Jamaica, when suddenly I get a fax that the dumb school was back open. Well, those kids better not bother me. My friends? That's a joke! Like I would really want to be friends with those little snot-nose— *What*? Don't tell me to shut up! You shut up! What's on? You mean they're hearing what I'm saying right this very second? Well, how do you turn it off? What button? I don't see a red button. There is no red button. Oh, here it

3. Poetry

Mrs. Jewls told everyone to pick a color and write a poem about it.

"Huh?" said Joy.

"For example," said Mrs. Jewls, "if brown was your favorite color, you might write: 'At the circus I saw a clown. On his face was a great big frown. His sad eyes were big and brown.' "

"Could you repeat that just a little bit slower?" asked Joy.

Mrs. Jewls repeated it for her.

"Ooh, I'm going to do purple!" said Rondi. Rondi loved anything purple.

"You can't do purple," said Allison. "I'm doing it."

"So?" said Rondi. "Mrs. Jewls didn't say two people couldn't do the same color."

"But purple is my favorite color in the world," said Allison.

Rondi and Allison were best friends, but Allison always got her way.

Rondi switched to blue.

Joe raised his hand. "I don't know what rhymes with red," he said.

Mrs. Jewls gave him a few suggestions. "Bed, led, wed. Think of words that end in 'e-d.' "

"Oh, I get it!" said Joe. He set to work.

Rondi tried to think of words that rhymed with blue. She raised her hand. "Mrs. Jewls!" she said. "I chose blue. Can I rhyme that with zoo?"

"Yes, that would be a good rhyme," agreed Mrs. Jewls.

"How about glue?" asked Rondi.

"Yes, that rhymes too," said Mrs. Jewls.

"Oh, I know!" said Rondi. "How about stew?"

"Just pick one and get started," said Mrs. Jewls.

Rondi smiled. "This is fun," she told Allison. "There are lots of words that rhyme with blue."

Allison grunted.

Nothing rhymed with purple. In her mind, Allison had gone through every letter of the alphabet: *aurple, burple, curple, durple* . . . all the way to *zurple.*

But after making a big stink over it with Rondi, she couldn't switch colors now.

Rondi was just about to start her poem when she got an even better idea: Love That's True. "Poets are always writing about Love That's True, aren't they, Mrs. Jewls?"

"Sometimes," said Mrs. Jewls.

Rondi smiled. Except she really didn't know much about true love.

"Morning dew!" she said. "Poets write about morning dew too, don't they, Mrs. Jewls?"

"I believe so," said Mrs. Jewls.

Dana walked to Mrs. Jewls's desk. "I can't think of anything that rhymes with pink," she complained.

"I'm sure you'll *think* of something," said Mrs. Jewls. She winked at her.

"I can't think," said Dana. "My mind's on the blink. I'm no good at poetry. I stink!"

"Just keep trying," said Mrs. Jewls.

13

Dana returned to her seat. She started to put her name on her paper, but her pen wouldn't write. "Great!" she complained. "Now my pen's out of ink!"

"Hey, Dana," whispered John. "Do you want to borrow my pen?"

"Sure," said Dana.

"Too bad, I'm using it," said John. Then he and Joe cracked up.

Meanwhile, Allison was going through the alphabet for the tenth time. . . . *Murple, nurple, ourple, qurple,* . . . she thought.

"My left shoe!" exclaimed Rondi.

"You better choose something, Rondi, and get started," advised Mrs. Jewls.

"I got it!" said Rondi. "A Bird That Flew!"

At the end of the day, the children turned in their poems.

Yellow
by Kathy

I don't feel too well, oh
I don't know who to tell, oh
I'm sick and I smell, oh
My barf is yellow

14

Green
by Stephen

The swimming pool has lots of chlorine.
It turned my hair green.

Brown
by Joy

At the circus I saw a clown.
On his face was a great big frown.
His sad eyes were big and brown.

Red
by Joe

The fire truck is red!
It hurried!
The siren wailed!
The house burned!
The firemen saved
The baby who screamed.

Pink
by Dana

My favorite color is pink.
John is a ratfink!

15

Purple
by Allison

The baby won't stop crying.
His face is turning purple.
Will anything make him feel better?
I bet a burp'll.

Blue
by Rondi

That was as far as she got.

4. Doctor Pickle

Actually his name was Doctor Pickell, with the accent on the second syllable. But that wasn't why everyone called him Dr. Pickle.

Dr. Pickle was a psychiatrist. He had thick eyebrows and wore tiny glasses. He had a small beard on the tip of his pointed chin.

A psychiatrist is a doctor who doesn't cure people with sick bodies. He cures people with sick minds.

Although Dr. Pickle had a pretty sick mind himself.

One day a woman came into his office. She smoked too much, and she wanted him to help her quit.

"I know that smoking is no good for me," she said as she puffed on her cigarette. "It's bad for my heart. It fills my lungs with gunk. And my husband won't kiss me because my breath stinks. But I can't quit!"

She finished her cigarette, smushed it out in an ashtray, then immediately lit another one.

"Have a seat," said Dr. Pickle.

She sat down on the couch.

"Look into my eyes," said Dr. Pickle.

The woman stared into his deep, penetrating eyes.

Dr. Pickle held up a gold chain. At the end of the chain was a green stone that was almost transparent, but not quite. It looked like a pickle.

Hence, his name.

"Watch the pickle," he said, as he gently moved the chain.

The pickle went back and forth, back and forth, back and forth.

The woman's eyes went back and forth, back and forth, back and forth.

"Put down your cigarette," Dr. Pickle said in a strong but gentle voice.

The woman set her cigarette in the ashtray as she continued to stare at the pickle.

"You are getting sleepy," said Dr. Pickle. "Your eyelids are getting heavy."

The woman blinked her eyes.

"When I count to three," said Dr. Pickle, "you will fall into a deep, deep sleep. One . . . two . . . three."

The woman's eyes closed.

Dr. Pickle put down the pickle. "Can you hear me?" he asked.

"Yes," said the woman, in a low voice from deep inside her.

"You will do what I say," said Dr. Pickle.

"I - will - do - what - you - say," the woman repeated.

"I am going to count to five," said Dr. Pickle. "And then you will wake up. And, as usual, you will want to smoke a cigarette."

"I - will - want - to - smoke - a - cigarette," the woman repeated.

"But when you put the cigarette in your mouth," said Dr. Pickle, "it will feel just like a worm. A wiggling, slimy worm."

"A - yucky - icky - worm," repeated the woman.

"Good," said Dr. Pickle. "Now just one more

thing." He rubbed his beard and smiled. "Whenever your husband says the word 'potato,' you will slap him across the face."

"When - Fred - says - 'potato' - I - will - slap - his - face."

"Good," said Dr. Pickle. He counted to five.

The woman woke up.

"So do you think you can help me?" she asked in her normal voice, as she reached for her cigarette.

Dr. Pickle shrugged.

She put her cigarette in her mouth, then screamed as she pulled it out.

She looked at the cigarette, puzzled. "Hm?" she said. She placed it back in her mouth, then spit it out onto the floor.

"I'm sorry," she said, a little confused. She picked up the cigarette and put it in the ashtray.

"That's all right," said Dr. Pickle.

She took out a new cigarette from her pack, but as soon as she put that in her mouth, she spit it out too.

"I'm sorry," she said again. "I don't know what's come over me."

She walked out of his office shaking her head. She dropped her pack of cigarettes in the trash.

She never smoked again.

It was an interesting thing about the word "potato." Whenever Fred said it, she slapped him. And he'd ask her why she slapped him, but she never remembered slapping him, so they'd get in a big fight, each calling the other crazy. Then they'd kiss and make up, which was nice because her breath didn't stink.

They never figured out it had anything to do with saying "potato." How could they?

But deep down they both must have realized it somehow, because while they used to eat lots of potatoes, they gradually ate fewer and fewer, until they finally stopped eating them altogether.

Dr. Pickle was a good doctor, but he kept playing those kinds of jokes on people. There was a woman who quacked like a duck whenever she saw a freight train with more than twenty cars. There was a man who took off his shoe anytime someone said "parking meter."

Eventually Dr. Pickle was caught, and he was no longer allowed to practice psychiatry. So he had to find another job.

He became a counselor at an elementary school.

5. A Story with a Disappointing Ending

Paul's father was a security guard at a museum. The museum had a very famous painting.

It was painted by Leonardo da Vinci. It was called the *Mona Lisa.*

Next to the painting was a sign.

DO NOT TOUCH!

All day Paul's father made sure nobody touched the painting.

At night, after the museum closed, Paul's father was alone. Just him and the *Mona Lisa.*

And the sign. Do not touch! Do not touch! Do not . . .

He was dying to touch it. The tips of his fingers tingled with desire.

But this story isn't about Paul's father. It's about Paul.

Paul was a student in Mrs. Jewls's class. He sat behind Leslie.

Leslie had two long brown pigtails that reached down to her waist. They just hung there, all day, right in front of Paul's face.

The Mona Leslie.

Do not touch! Do not touch! Do not . . .

Paul reached out, grabbed, and yanked!

"Yaaaaaaaahhhhhhhh!" screamed Leslie.

Mrs. Jewls sent Paul to the counselor's office.

The counselor's office was on the fourth floor. Paul had never been there before.

Like every student in Wayside School, he was afraid of the counselor. The counselor had a very scary face, with big, bushy eyebrows and a little beard on his pointed chin.

Paul knocked on the door.

"Come in," said the counselor.

Paul entered and sat down on the couch.

"What's the problem?" asked the counselor.

"I pulled Leslie's pigtails again," said Paul. "I know it's wrong, but I just can't help myself."

"Watch the pickle," said the counselor.

Paul's eyes went back and forth as he stared at the swaying pickle.

"You are getting sleepy," said the counselor. "Your eyelids are getting heavy."

Paul suddenly felt very tired. He could hardly keep his eyes open.

"When I count to three," said the counselor, "you will fall into a deep, deep sleep. One . . . two . . . three."

Paul closed his eyes. He wasn't exactly asleep. He felt like he was living in a dream. But it was a very pleasant dream. He felt happy and safe.

"Can you hear me?" asked the counselor.

"Yes," said Paul. He was no longer afraid of the counselor. In fact, he liked him a lot.

"You will do what I say," said the counselor.

"I - will - do - what - you - say," Paul repeated.

"I am going to count to five," said the counselor. "And then you will wake up. You will return to your classroom. You will take your seat behind Leslie. You will want to pull one of her pigtails. But when you reach for it, it will turn into a rattle-snake."

"Leslie's - pigtails - are - rattlesnakes," said Paul.

"Very good," said the counselor. "Now just one more thing." He rubbed his beard and smiled.

"When Leslie says the word 'pencil,' her ears will turn into candy. The most delicious candy in the world. The candy of your dreams."

Paul licked his lips. He could almost taste the rich chocolate and chewy caramel.

"And you will try to eat the candy."

"When - Leslie - says - 'pencil' - I - will - eat - her - ears," said Paul.

The counselor counted to five.

Paul's eyes blinked open.

"You may go back to class now," said the counselor.

"I'm not in trouble?" asked Paul.

"No," said the counselor.

Paul shrugged. He returned to class. As he passed Leslie, she stuck out her tongue at him.

He sat down behind her.

"What'd the counselor do to you?" asked Eric Fry.

"Nothing," said Paul. "He's a nice man."

He looked at Leslie's pigtails. He had pulled

the one on the left. But he still wanted to pull the one on the right.

He lunged for it.

It hissed at him. Its tail rattled.

He screamed and fell back over in his chair.

Everyone laughed.

"Paul, are you all right?" asked Mrs. Jewls.

"Uh, I guess so," said Paul, getting back up.

He didn't feel much like pulling Leslie's pig-tails anymore.

It was just a short while later that Leslie's pencil point broke.

"Oh, great!" she complained.

"What's the matter?" asked Jenny, who sat next to Leslie.

Leslie showed her the broken pencil point.

"You want to borrow mine?" asked Eric Fry, who sat behind Jenny.

"No, I'll just go sharpen it," said Leslie. She went to the back of the room and sharpened her pencil.

She returned to her seat. She set the pencil on her desk, but it rolled off when she sat down.

"Hey, where'd it go?" she asked, turning around.

"Where'd what go?" asked Paul.

"There it is," said Jenny. "Under Paul's desk."

"What's under my desk?" asked Paul.

"I'll get it," said Eric Fry. He reached under Paul's desk, picked up the pencil, and handed it to Leslie.

She thanked him and everyone returned to work.

6. Pet Day

All the kids in Mrs. Jewls's class brought a pet to school. The room was very noisy. Dogs barked. Cats meowed. A frog croaked. A pig squealed. A cow mooed. Birds tweeted.

Mrs. Jewls held up two fingers.

All the animals became quiet.

Stephen didn't have a pet. So he brought an orange. He kept it in a cage on his desk so it couldn't escape.

Todd brought Ralphie, his baby brother.

"Todd?" said Mrs. Jewls.

Todd barked.

"You cannot have a pet human," said Mrs. Jewls.

"He doesn't bite," Todd assured her.

Joy told Todd to sit and be quiet.

Mrs. Jewls got a large piece of poster board from the supply closet. "Let's make a chart," she said.

Across the top of her chart she wrote, "Name of Kid," "Kind of Pet," "Name of Pet."

She started with Deedee. She wrote "Deedee" under "Name of Kid." "And you have a dog," she said.

"Cat," said Deedee.

"Cat?" asked Mrs. Jewls.

Deedee nodded as she petted her dog.

Mrs. Jewls moved on to Ron. "Ron, I see you have a cat."

"Dog," said Ron, as he stroked the cat on his lap.

Mrs. Jewls shrugged. "Okay," she said.

"He's my dog," said D.J.

"Ron has your dog?" asked Mrs. Jewls.

"Ron has a cat," said D.J.

"That's what I thought," said Mrs. Jewls. "But what—"

"What's a dog," said Jenny.

Mrs. Jewls covered her ears and shook her head. "Let's start all over again," said Mrs. Jewls. She got a new piece of poster board from the supply closet.

"Mac, what's your dog's name?"

"What's my dog's name," said Jenny.

"I'm not talking to you, Jenny. I'm talking to Mac."

"He can't talk," said Mac.

"Who can't talk?" asked Mrs. Jewls.

"Mac," said Mac.

Billy barked at Mac.

Mac barked at Billy.

Todd barked at both of them.

Joy made Todd lie down by her feet.

Mrs. Jewls moved on. "What's your pet, Myron?" she asked.

"Your pet's a turtle," said Sharie.

"What?" asked Mrs. Jewls.

"What is Jenny's pet," said Sharie.

"Jenny's pet is a dog!" said Mrs. Jewls. "What's his name, Jenny?"

Jenny nodded. Her dog sat up straight and tall and seemed to smile at Mrs. Jewls.

"He's handsome," said Mrs. Jewls.

"My mouse is handsome," said Benjamin.

Benjamin had a little white mouse in a cage on his desk.

"If you like mice," said Dana, making a face.

"Mrs. Jewls likes mice," said Calvin. "She eats them."

"Gross!" said Dana.

"He won't come when you call him," said Kathy. "He doesn't know his name."

Billy meowed.

"Will Mrs. Jewls eat yogurt?" asked John.

"No way!" said Calvin.

"I will too," said Mrs. Jewls. "I like yogurt. I like strawberry best."

Maurecia beamed. "Mrs. Jewls likes strawberry best," she bragged.

"You shouldn't pick favorites," complained Dana.

"Do you like crackers, Mrs. Jewls?" asked Rondi.

"Don't worry," said Calvin. "Mrs. Jewls won't eat crackers."

"How do you know what I'll eat, Calvin?" asked Mrs. Jewls, a little annoyed. "I like eating crackers with cheese on top."

"Oh, gross!" said Myron.

"He won't come when you call him," Kathy said again.

"Mac! Keep Mac away from my socks!" shouted Allison.

"Wait," said Jason. "Now you've got my socks, and I've got your socks."

"I can tell the difference between my socks and your socks, Jason," said Allison.

Mrs. Jewls covered her ears and shook her head. She moved on. "What's your pet, Dameon?" she asked.

"I already told you he was a turtle," said Sharie.

"I wasn't talking to you, Sharie," said Mrs. Jewls. "I was talking to Dameon."

"Your nose a ferret," said Dameon.

"My nose a ferret?" asked Mrs. Jewls.

"My nose a hamster," said Joe.

Billy bleated.

Mrs. Jewls licked her leg.

"Hey, Paul," said Leslie. "I like your pigtails."

"Thanks," said Paul. "May I touch your pajamas?"

"Go ahead," said Bebe, who was already petting Leslie's pajamas. "She won't scratch you."

"This is crazy!" shouted Terrence.

"He's cute," said Dana.

Name of Kid	Kind of Pet	Name of Pet
Deedee	Dog	Cat
Ron	Cat	Dog
D. J.	Dog	O.K.
Jenny	Dog	What
Mac	Dog	Mac
Joy	Dog	Todd
Sharie	Turtle	Yorpet
Benjamin	Mouse	Handsome
Calvin	Cat	Mrs. Jewls
Kathy	Skunk	Gross
John	Frog	Yogurt
Maurecia	Cat	Strawberry
Rondi	Bird	Crackers
Myron	Chipmunk	Cheese
Allison	Cat	Socks
Jason	Cat	Socks
Dameon	Ferret	Yorno
Joe	Hamster	Mino
Paul	Pig	Tails
Leslie	Cat	Pajamas
Terrence	Dog	Crazy
Eric Fry	Kid (Goat)	Billy
Eric Bacon	Dog	Billy
Eric Ovens	Cat	Billy
Dana	Dog	Pugsy
Bebe	Bird	Picasso
Todd	Kid (Human)	Ralphie
Stephen	Orange	Fido

7. A Bad Word

Early in the morning, a white limousine drove up to Wayside School.

Just like always.

The chauffeur got out of the car, then opened the passenger door.

Just like always.

Mr. Kidswatter stepped out of the car. "Thank you, James," he said.

"My name is David," said the chauffeur.

Just like always.

Mr. Kidswatter entered the school building.

"Good morning, Mr. Kidswatter," said Mrs. Day, the school secretary. She handed him a cup of hot coffee.

Just like always.

"Thank you, Miss Night," said Mr. Kidswatter.

He walked into his office.

Except his office door was closed.

He smashed into it, spilling coffee all over his green suit.

"Who closed my door?" he demanded.

"Why didn't you just open it?" asked Mrs. Day.

"It's *always* open in the morning," said Mr. Kidswatter. "How was I supposed to know it was closed *this time*?"

Up on the thirtieth story, Mrs. Jewls took roll.

Todd was absent.

"Oh dear, I hope Todd is all right," said Mrs. Jewls.

"Todd's never all right!" said Joy.

She and Maurecia laughed.

Dameon looked at Mrs. Jewls. Ever since he returned to Wayside School, he'd thought there was something *different* about her, but he still couldn't figure out what it was.

Mr. Kidswatter's voice came over the P.A. system. **"Good morning, boys and girls."**

There was the usual pause.

"Today I want to talk about doors," said Mr. Kidswatter.

"This should be interesting," said Mrs. Jewls.

"Do you know how many doors there are in this school building?" asked Mr. Kidswatter.

Mrs. Jewls shook her head.

"Well, there are a lot! Over thirty! And some of you probably have doors at home too. Maybe more than one. All those doors. Think about it."

"Well, Mr. Kidswatter has certainly given us something to think about this morning," said Mrs. Jewls.

"So remember," said Mr. Kidswatter. **"And please be careful! Always check to see if a door is open before going through it. And if it's not open, open it. If you can't open it yourself, ask someone to open it for you. This may not make a lot of sense to you now, but someday you'll thank me."**

Mrs. Jewls looked around the class. "That's good advice," she said. "I think most of you already knew it, but at least it's nice to know we have a principal who cares."

"I hate doors!" shouted Mr. Kidswatter. **"It's**

a dumb word. Door. Door. Door. Who made up that word, anyway?"

Mrs. Jewls waited a little longer, but Mr. Kidswatter seemed to be finished. "Some people just don't like doors," she said.

"I have made a new rule!" declared Mr. Kidswatter. **"You may no longer say that word. You know what word I mean—but don't say it! Instead, I have made up a new word for you: 'Goozack.' Open the goozack. Shut the goozack. Lock the goozack. Don't you think that's a better word? I do. From now on, that other word is a bad word. I have made my decision."**

Everyone turned around and looked at the goozack.

Suddenly it opened.

Todd entered. "I'm sorry I'm late," he said.

"That's okay," said Mrs. Jewls. "I'm just glad you're not sick or hurt."

"My dad locked his keys in the car," Todd explained. "We had to use a coat hanger to unlock the door."

Everyone gasped.

Mrs. Jewls made Todd write his name on the blackboard under the word DISCIPLINE.

8. Santa Claus

'Twas the last day of school
Before winter vacation,
And the children were having
A small celebration.

Their artwork was hung
By the blackboards with pride:
Snowmen, and mooses,
And a joyful sleigh ride.

They ate homemade cookies,
  (Red and green ones, of course.)
When Kathy declared,
  "I don't believe in Santa Claus!"

She just opened her mouth,
  And said what she said.
"Santa Claus isn't real,
  And besides that, he's dead!

"So you bet I will pout,
  And you bet I will cry.
"You bet I will shout,
  I'm telling you why. . . ."

Stephen covered his ears. "No, you're wrong!" he shouted. "It's not true. There is a Santa Claus. I know there is!"

"Ho, ho, ho," laughed Kathy.

"Kathy is just saying that because she never gets any presents," said Jason.

"All she ever gets is a lump of coal!" said Rondi.

"Wrong!" said Kathy. "I get lots of presents. My parents buy them for me. They have lots of money. They buy me anything I want."

She bit off the head of a reindeer cookie. "The

only thing that matters is how rich your parents are. If they have lots of money, then you'll get lots of good presents. If they're poor, then you'll just get a few crummy presents."

Everyone tried to argue with her, but Kathy just asked them all the old questions, like "How does a fat man fit down a skinny chimney?" or "How could he visit everyone's house in the whole world in one night?"

And of course nobody knew the answers. Nobody ever has.

"Only Santa knows the answers to those questions," said Rondi.

"Don't you even like Christmas?" asked Stephen.

"Sure," said Kathy.

"I get lots of presents,
And I don't have to work."
Then she stuck out her tongue
and called Stephen a jerk.

Poor Stephen sputtered
As his face turned quite blue,
"If you don't believe in Santa,
He won't believe in you!"

But Kathy just yelped.
   "You know that it's true!
Do you still believe in the Easter bunny,
   The tooth fairy, and Miss Zarves too?"

"Let's ask Mrs. Jewls!" said Maurecia.
   "She's a teacher who's wise.
Let's ask Mrs. Jewls.
   She never lies!"

The children crowded round
   Their wise teacher's desk
And asked her the question
   Never found on a test.

"Is there a Santa?
   You're a teacher with smarts!
Is Santa Claus real?"
   They asked with pure hearts.

And oh, Mrs. Jewls,
   That teacher so wise,
Looked at their faces
   And bright, eager eyes.

She had to say something.
 It was her job to reply.
"Tell them," yelped Kathy.
 "That reindeer can't fly!"

Outside the window
 Snowflakes were falling. . . .
Inside the window
 Mrs. Jewls was stalling. . . .

"Are our parents all liars?"
 "Is it all just a trick
To make us be good
 For fear of St. Nick?"

"Tell us the truth;
 Don't try to fake it.
Is there a Santa?
 Let us know; we can take it."

Mrs. Jewls cleared her throat,
 Then she cleared it again.
She put down her pencil.
 She picked up her pen.

"Hey, look!" shouted Leslie.
  "Look there! Who's that?
Someone is coming in
  Through the goozack!"

Sure enough, the door opened.
  It had to open quite wide!
As a strange-looking stranger
  Stepped sideways inside.

He wore a red suit
  And had a white, fluffy beard.
And even for Wayside
  He looked pretty weird!

His fat belly shook
  Like a bowl full of Jell-O.
There was no doubt about it.
  They knew that fellow!

It was Louis, the yard teacher.

"What are you doing in that stupid suit, Louis?" asked Sharie. "Aren't you hot?"

"Why are you wearing a fake beard?" asked Todd.

"Is that a pillow under your jacket?" asked Jason.

Kathy was delighted. "See!" she said. "That proves there's no Santa Claus! If there was, Louis wouldn't have to dress up like a fool and pretend to be him."

"I'm not Louis," said Louis. "I'm Santa Claus. Ho! Ho—"

"You're lying to us, Louis," said John. "Everyone is always lying to us. Kathy's right. Christmas is nothing but a dirty, stinking lie!"

"I was just trying to bring a little holiday cheer," said Louis.

"Go home, Jerome," said Terrence.

"Now, that's no way to talk to Louis," said Mrs. Jewls. "Louis is one of Santa's special helpers."

"Really, Louis?" asked Deedee.

Louis looked at Mrs. Jewls. "That's right," he said.

The children were all very impressed.

"Have you ever met him?" demanded Kathy.

"Well, no, not exactly," Louis admitted.

"See!" said Kathy. "It's just another lie."

"You don't have to meet Santa to be one of his special helpers," said Mrs. Jewls.

"Then how do you know what he wants you to do?" asked John.

44

"That's easy," said Mrs. Jewls. "You just have to be nice to other people. Whenever you give someone a present or sing a holiday song, you're helping Santa Claus. To me, that's what Christmas is all about. Helping Santa Claus!"

"Can I be one of his helpers?" asked Dameon.

"You bet," said Mrs. Jewls.

"Hey, everybody," shouted Dameon. "I'm one of Santa's helpers!"

"Me too," said Allison.

"There must be a Santa Claus!" cheered Stephen. "Because it feels so good to help him."

So the children all helped Santa,
*   In every way they could,*
By singing songs and giving gifts
*   And just by being good.*

"But there is no Santa Claus!"
*   Kathy continued to yelp.*
"Well, if that's the case," said Mrs. Jewls.
*   "He must really need our help."*

9. Something Different about Mrs. Jewls

The children returned from Christmas vacation. On each desk were two knitting needles and a hunk of yarn.

"Today we are going to learn how to knit," said Mrs. Jewls.

She showed the class how it was done. "See, you stick this needle through here, then wrap this around this like this, stick this through this, pull this like this, and then you stick this here. Any questions?"

Everyone stared at her.

"Good," said Mrs. Jewls. "I want everybody to make socks. Okay, get started."

Dameon looked at his knitting needles. He didn't have a clue.

He looked back at Mrs. Jewls. Now, more than ever, he was sure she was somehow *different.*

She was sitting at her desk, knitting and eating Baloneos. Dameon couldn't remember Mrs. Jewls ever eating a Baloneo before.

A Baloneo was an Oreo cookie, except instead of the white part, there was a round hunk of baloney.

Miss Mush invented them.

"Hey, Mac," whispered Dameon. "Does Mrs. Jewls seem different to you?"

"She's fat," said Mac.

"That's not a nice thing to say," said Dameon.

"I didn't say it to Mrs. Jewls," said Mac. "I didn't go, 'Hey, Mrs. Jewls. You're fat!' "

Mrs. Jewls cleared her throat as she stood up. She walked around the room. "Very nice, D.J.," she said. "You're doing fine, Rondi."

She stopped at Joe's desk.

"Oh, Joe!" she gushed. "Look, everybody, I want you to see Joe's sock!" She held it up. "Isn't it the most beautiful sock you ever saw?"

It was a great sock. Everybody oohed and aahed.

Joe was as surprised as anyone. He didn't know he knew how to make socks. But the boy was born to knit.

Mrs. Jewls started to cry. "I love this sock," she sobbed.

"Uh-oh," said Kathy. "I think she's finally flipped out!"

"I love you, Kathy," said Mrs. Jewls. She looked around the room. "I love all of you."

She put her hand on Kathy's desk. "I love this desk," she said. "I love the blackboard. I love the clock on the wall."

There was a ruler on the floor.

Mrs. Jewls picked it up. "I love this ruler," she declared.

"Hey, that's mine!" said Dana. "But, uh, that's okay, Mrs. Jewls. You can have it."

"I don't want your ruler, Dana," said Mrs. Jewls, handing it to her.

"You want my pair of scissors?" offered Sharie.

"Don't give her anything sharp!" warned Kathy.

Mrs. Jewls wiped away her tears and smiled at the class. "I'm going to miss all of you very much," she said.

"Are you going away?" asked Dameon.

"Yeah, to the loony bin," whispered Kathy.

"Are you sick?" asked Eric Ovens.

"No, I'm not sick," said Mrs. Jewls. "In fact, I'm better than I've ever been." She beamed. "I'm going to have a baby!"

Everyone gasped.

Dameon couldn't believe it! He was so happy he jumped out of his seat and hugged Mrs. Jewls.

She was soon surrounded by all her students, even Kathy, wanting to hug her.

"Today is my last day here," Mrs. Jewls told her students. "My doctor doesn't want me walking up and down thirty flights of stairs every day. I wasn't even supposed to come today, but I just had to say good-bye."

"I thought you were getting fat," said Mac. "But I didn't want to say anything."

"Thank you, Mac," said Mrs. Jewls. "You are very considerate."

"Can I touch your stomach?" asked Stephen.

Mrs. Jewls laughed. "Sure," she said.

The children took turns touching her stomach.

"What are you going to name your baby?" asked Allison.

"I don't know yet," said Mrs. Jewls. "What do you think?"

"Well, if she's a girl," said Allison, "I think you should name her Rainbow Sunshine."

"That's a nice name," said Mrs. Jewls. "And if he's a boy?"

"Bucket Head," said Allison. She didn't like boys.

"If he's a boy, you should name him Jet Rocket!" said Joe.

"Jet Rocket Jewls," mused Mrs. Jewls. "That has a nice ring to it. And what if she's a girl?"

"Cootie Face," said Joe.

Mrs. Jewls laughed. "So let me get this straight," she said. "If he's a boy, I'll name him Bucket Head."

"Right," said Allison and Rondi.

"And if she's a girl, I'll name her Cootie Face."

"Right," said Joe and John.

Dameon laughed. He knew Mrs. Jewls was only joking. At least he hoped she was.

Terrence placed his palm flat against Mrs. Jewls's stomach. "Hey," he exclaimed. "The dude kicked me!"

Suddenly Dameon felt very sad. He was going to miss her a lot! He wiped a tear from his eye. "It's unfair!" he shouted. "We finally come back to Wayside School after being gone for so long. And now you're leaving us!"

"I have to," said Mrs. Jewls.

"I know," whined Dameon. "You have to make sure that you and your baby are healthy. But it still isn't fair!"

"I think you'll like your substitute teacher," said Mrs. Jewls. "I spoke to him over the vacation. He seems like a very nice man."

"A man?" asked Dameon. "Cool!"

They all thought it was pretty neat to have a man teacher.

"Yes," said Mrs. Jewls. "His name is Mr. Gorf."

10. Mr. Gorf

"Mr. Gorf," muttered Joy as she walked down the stairs to recess. "Did she say Mr. Gorf?"

Maurecia nodded.

Leslie caught up to them. "Did she say Mr. Gorf?"

"I think so," said Maurecia.

"Do you think—?" Leslie asked.

"I don't know," said Maurecia.

"I hope not," said Joy.

Before Mrs. Jewls ever came to Wayside

School, the children had a teacher named Mrs. Gorf. She wasn't very nice.

Even Myron was worried. And Myron had never gotten in trouble in his whole life.

"Mr. Gorf might be a good teacher," said Eric Bacon. "Just because he has the same last name as Mrs. Gorf doesn't mean he'll be horrible."

"That's right," said Eric Ovens. "People with the same name can be different."

"I agree," said Eric Fry.

"There are probably lots of people named Gorf," Dameon said hopefully. "I bet if you looked in the phone book, you'd find ten whole pages of Gorfs."

"Well, I don't know about you, but I'm not coming to school tomorrow," said Joy.

"Me neither," Maurecia agreed.

But the next morning their parents made them all go to school.

Everyone arrived on time. Nobody dared to be late.

But there was no teacher.

Deedee sat down next to Myron. "Is he here?" she whispered.

"Sh!" whispered Myron. He folded his hands on his desk and stared straight ahead.

One by one, the children entered the class-room and quietly sat down at their desks.

They couldn't take any chances. Mr. Gorf might walk through the door any moment. Or maybe he was already there, hiding in the coat closet, just waiting for someone to do something wrong.

"I didn't want to come today," whispered Calvin. "But my parents made me."

"Sh!" said Bebe. "He might hear you."

Mr. Kidswatter's voice came over the P.A. system. **"Good morning, boys and girls."**

"Good morning, Mr. Kidswatter," the children all answered together, like good little boys and girls.

They listened attentively to their principal. Then, when Mr. Kidswatter was finished, they took out their arithmetic books and started working.

After that, they did social studies, reading, and spelling.

When the recess bell rang, the children put their books neatly in their desks, quietly lined up, and walked out of the room and down the stairs.

"So how's your substitute teacher?" asked Louis, out on the playground.

"Tough!" said Bebe. "I've never worked so hard in my life."

"I did more work before ten o'clock than most people do in a day," said Calvin.

"But he's very fair," Myron quickly added, just in case Mr. Gorf was listening. He might have been hiding in the bushes.

"Yes, he's nice and fair and a very good teacher," said Jenny.

"Very smart too," said Deedee. "We're lucky to have him."

Louis twisted the end of his mustache between his fingers.

After recess the children returned to class and worked until lunchtime. At lunch they ate all the food Miss Mush served them. Their manners were perfect.

Mr. Gorf might have been hiding under the table.

After lunch they returned to class and practiced their handwriting.

Myron looked around. All of a sudden he got a terrible urge to do something. Anything!

"Ugga bugga," he said.

Jenny put her finger to her lips.

"Biff. Boff. Boof!" said Myron, a little louder.

"Sh!" said Jenny.

Myron stood up. "No!" he shouted. "I don't have to be quiet!"

Everyone tried to get Myron to hush up.

Myron climbed on top of his desk. "Look around, folks! There's no teacher! We're doing all this work for nothing!"

"Get down!" whispered Allison. "Do you want to get us all in trouble?"

Myron jumped on top of Allison's desk. "Hi, Allison!" he said. Then he hopped over to Deedee's desk, then Ron's, then Maurecia's.

"Please, Myron," said Maurecia.

"This is fun!" said Myron. He made a great leap and landed on top of the teacher's desk.

Mrs. Jewls had always kept a coffee can full of Tootsie Roll Pops on her desk. It was still there.

"Hey, anyone want a Tootsie Roll Pop?" asked Myron.

Everyone stared at him.

Myron took one for himself. He sat in the teacher's chair, with his feet up on the teacher's desk, and sucked on it.

"Please stop, Myron!" begged Jenny. "What if he's hiding in the closet?"

"Get real!" said Myron. "Why would he hide in the closet?"

"What if Mr. Gorf was married to Mrs. Gorf?" asked Allison.

Myron laughed. "Who would ever want to marry Mrs. Gorf?" he asked.

"Somebody had to marry her," said Rondi. "Or else she wouldn't have been a Mrs."

"What if he loved her very much?" asked Allison. "And then one day she didn't come home from work. And he never saw her again. And he didn't know what happened to her. But he knew she used to teach this class! So he might be hiding in the closet to try to find out if we're the ones who got rid of her."

"If I was married to Mrs. Gorf," said Jason, "I'd be glad she never came home. He should thank us."

"Nice going, Jason!" said Jenny. "If he *is* hiding in the closet, you just told him we're the ones who got rid of his wife."

"Well, if I didn't, you just did," said Jason.

"It doesn't matter!" shouted Myron. "Because Mr. Gorf is not hiding in the closet!"

Myron went to the back of the room and opened the closet door.

A man stepped out. "Thank you," he said. "I accidentally locked myself in here this morning, and I've been waiting for someone to open the door."

Myron swallowed his Tootsie Roll Pop, stick and all.

11. Voices

"My name is Mr. Gorf," said the man who stepped out of the closet.

And, surprising as it may seem, the children weren't afraid.

It was his voice. His voice was full of comfort and wisdom, like an old leather chair in a dusty library. It didn't matter what he said. It felt good just to listen to him.

He was a handsome man, with neatly combed brown hair and clean fingernails. He carried a brown briefcase.

Nobody even noticed that his nose had three nostrils.

"Since I am going to be your teacher for the next few months, let me tell you a bit about myself. I was born in the Himalayan Mountains in a town called Katmandu."

"Cat Man Do," said Terrence. "Cool."

Everyone laughed. They weren't laughing at Terrence. There was just something about the name of that city and the way Terrence said it.

Terrence's voice was like a rusty drainpipe.

"Have you ever been married?" asked Allison. Allison's voice was like a cat walking across a piano.

"No, I'm a bachelor," said Mr. Gorf.

Allison smiled, greatly relieved.

"Well, that's enough about me," said Mr. Gorf. "How about some of you telling me about your-selves?"

"My name is Mac," said Mac, without raising his hand. Mac's voice was like a freight train. "I built the biggest snowman you ever saw. Man, it was huge. I had to stand on a ladder to put the hat on his head. It was a stovepipe hat, like Abraham Lincoln wore, but I don't know why they call it that. We have a microwave oven. Have you ever put a bag of marshmallows in a microwave oven? Man, it's like—"

Mr. Gorf's nose flared.

His right nostril flared to the right. His left nostril flared to the left. And the hole in the middle seemed to get larger.

Mac coughed. He tried to speak, but no words came out.

"Thank you, Mac," said Mr. Gorf. "Anyone else?"

Deedee raised her hand.

"Yes, young lady," said Mr. Gorf.

Deedee giggled. She liked the way he said "young lady." "My name is Deedee," she said. Her voice was small, but full of energy, like a superball. "I like soccer and Ninja Turtles. My favorite—"

Mr. Gorf's nose flared.

Deedee lost her voice too.

"Who's next?" asked Mr. Gorf. "Yes, the girl in the polka-dot shirt."

"My name's Maurecia," said Maurecia. "I have two brothers and one sister."

Maurecia's voice was like a pineapple milkshake.

Mr. Gorf sucked it up through his nose.

"Hey, what's going—," said Todd.

Todd was silent.

"Look at his nose!" shouted Eric Bacon. "It has—"

Eric Bacon had nothing else to say.

"Nobody say anyth—," Jenny tried to warn. Her voice disappeared up Mr. Gorf's nose.

Soon the class was quiet.

Mr. Gorf's middle nostril had snorted all of their voices.

Except for Allison. She remained silent. She knew she'd only get one chance to speak, and she had to wait for just the right moment.

"What good little boys and girls you are," said Mr. Gorf. "So nice and quiet." He laughed.

"Of course, this isn't my real voice," he said. "I stole this voice from a gentleman I met in Scotland."

He touched the tip of his nose.

"This is my voice!" he squawked.

If a donkey could talk, and if the donkey had a sore throat, and if it spoke with a French accent—that was what Mr. Gorf's voice sounded like.

But what he said next was even more horrible than his voice.

"Mrs. Gorf was my mommy."

The children sat frozen in their chairs, too scared to move.

Suddenly there was a knock on the door.

Mr. Gorf touched his nose. "Who is it?" he

61

asked in the pleasant voice he stole from the Scottish gentleman.

"Miss Mush," said Miss Mush from the other side of the door. "I just came up to say hello and welcome you to Wayside School."

"That's very nice of you, Miss Mush," said Mr. Gorf. "But we're very busy right now. Maybe we can get together for tea and crumpets sometime."

Miss Mush giggled. "That sounds lovely," she said. "By the way, Mr. Gorf, are you married?"

"No, I'm single," said Mr. Gorf.

"So am I," said Miss Mush.

"Miss Mush!" shouted Allison. "Help! Mr. Gorf is taking—"

Mr. Gorf's nose flared.

"Did you say something, Allison?" asked Miss Mush.

Mr. Gorf touched his nose. Then he spoke, this time using Allison's voice. "Mr. Gorf is taking us on a field trip next week. But he might need help. Do you want to come with us?"

"Maybe," said Miss Mush. "Thank you, Allison."

"Oh, don't thank me," said Allison's voice. "Thank Mr. Gorf. He's the best teacher in the whole world!"

"I'm glad," said Miss Mush. "He sounds very charming."

"And so do you," said Mr. Gorf, speaking like the gentleman from Scotland. He touched his nose.

"See you later, Miss Mush," said the voice of Eric Ovens.

"Take care," said Calvin's voice.

"Have a nice day," said Kathy's voice.

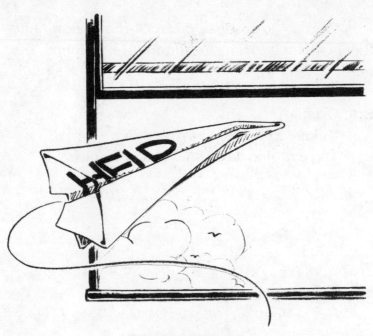

12. Nose

Mr. Gorf locked the door. "I don't want any more interruptions," he said.

Very quietly, Leslie slipped a piece of paper out of her desk. Then she felt around for a pencil.

Mr. Gorf returned to the teacher's desk. He opened the top drawer and took out the class list. It had the names of all the children in the class, their parents' names, and their parents' home and work phone numbers.

"Let's play a game!" he said, speaking in his

own, normal, French-donkey-with-a-sore-throat voice. "The name of the game is Who Am I Now?"

Leslie found a pencil. She held the piece of paper on her lap, where Mr. Gorf couldn't see it, and wrote HELP in big letters. She had to get it to Louis, the yard teacher.

Mr. Gorf touched the tip of his nose. "Who am I now?" he asked.

It was a girl's voice, soft and warm, with just a little bit of a giggle in it.

Everyone looked at Rondi.

"Rondi," said Mr. Gorf. He opened his briefcase and removed a portable phone. He dialed Rondi's home number.

"Hello, Mommy," Mr. Gorf said into the phone, using Rondi's voice. "No, nothing's wrong. I just called to say I hate you! You're the worst mommy in the whole world. You're ugly and you smell bad! It's not fair! Out of all the mommies in the world, I got stuck with you!"

He hung up the phone.

Rondi sat crying in her chair.

Mr. Gorf touched his nose. "Isn't this a good game?" he asked, sounding very much like a sick French donkey. "Rondi is crying. And at home, her mother is crying too." He laughed. "Too bad you won't ever be able to tell her you're sorry, Rondi."

Leslie carefully folded the piece of paper into a paper airplane. There was one open window, next to Sharie's desk.

Mr. Gorf touched his nose. "Who am I now?" he asked.

Everyone tried not to look at Joe.

Mr. Gorf called Joe's mother at work. "Hello, Mommy," he said. "I hate you! I wish you'd go away forever! Then maybe Daddy will marry somebody good this time."

Leslie knew she'd only have one chance. It would take a perfect throw. She tossed the paper airplane toward the window.

Mr. Gorf saw it. "Hey!" he shouted.

The airplane sailed closer . . . closer . . . but then at the last second it made a sudden turn, hit the wall, and landed on the floor.

Mr. Gorf laughed. He picked up the airplane and unfolded it. "Help," he sneered. "No one can help you now! You took my mommy away from me. And I'm going to take your mommies away from you!"

He touched his nose.

"Who am I now?" he asked.

It was Leslie's voice.

He started to dial her home phone number but was interrupted by a knock on the door.

"Oh, Mr. Gorf!" sang Miss Mush.

"Yes," said Mr. Gorf, still in Leslie's voice. He touched his nose and cleared his throat. "I mean, yes?" This time he sounded like a donkey with tonsillitis. He touched his nose again. "Yes?" he asked in the pleasant voice he took from the Scottish gentleman.

"It's me again," said Miss Mush. Miss Mush's voice was like two boots sloshing through mud. "I baked you a pie, Mr. Gorf. To welcome you to Wayside School."

Mr. Gorf sighed. "You are very kind, Miss Mush," he said. "But we are all quite busy at the moment. Perhaps another—"

"It's best to eat it while it's still warm," said Miss Mush. "You probably don't get fresh pies very often. Being a bachelor and all."

"I really hate to disturb the class," said Mr. Gorf. "I'll tell you what. I'll just come outside a moment, and you can hand it to me."

He glared at the class, daring them to move. Then he opened the door.

"I hope you like pepper pie," said Miss Mush. She smashed it in his face.

Mr. Gorf turned around. His face was covered with a thick pepper cream. He sneezed.

Calvin laughed.

"Hey, my voice is back!" said Calvin. "Wait a second. This isn't my voice. I sound like Bebe!"

Mr. Gorf sneezed again.

"I can talk!" shouted Jenny. "But who am I?"

Mr. Gorf sneezed.

"You're Maurecia!" said Jason. Jason sounded like the gentleman from Scotland.

Mr. Gorf kept sneezing.

"Who might I be, sonny?" Paul cackled. He sounded like somebody's grandmother.

Todd barked.

"AAAACHOOOO!!!!!!"

Mr. Gorf sneezed so hard his nose flew off his face. He screamed like a donkey, then ran nose-less out of the room.

"Oh, gross!" said Jason. "Now I sound like Allison."

Bebe said something in Italian.

"Nobody panic," said Miss Mush. "Your voices are bouncing around, trying to find where they belong. It might take a while, but soon you will be back to normal."

"How do you know?" asked Leslie, although she sounded like Paul. "And how'd you know to smash a pepper pie in Mr. Gorf's face?"

"I wasn't exactly sure," explained Miss Mush. "But when I came up the first time, I heard Kathy

68

say 'Have a nice day.' So, either Kathy had decided to be nice to me, or Mr. Gorf was a mean teacher who sucked children's voices up his nose." She shrugged. "I just didn't think Kathy would be nice."

"Maybe if you learned to brush your teeth," muttered Kathy.

Mr. Gorf's nose lay on the floor. Miss Mush picked it up and put it in her apron pocket. "It will go good in spaghetti sauce," she said.

Soon all the children had their real voices back. Rondi and Joe called their mothers on Mr. Gorf's portable phone and told them they loved them.

While far away, in a small village in Scotland, a man who hadn't spoken for twenty years turned to his wife and said, "Top of the morning to you, Tilly."

13. The New Teacher

The new teacher entered the classroom carrying a big blue notebook stuffed with papers. She had white hair and wore glasses. She was a lot older than anyone else in the class.

She took a big breath. "My, it's tiring walking up all those stairs, isn't it?" she said.

Nobody said anything. They just stared at her.

She set her notebook on the teacher's desk. "My name is Mrs. Drazil," she said. "And I'm not from Brazil." She smiled at her little joke.

Nobody else smiled. After Mrs. and Mr. Gorf, they didn't trust teachers.

Drazil, thought Deedee. *Where have I heard that name before?*

"Where are you from?" asked Leslie.

"Actually, I was born not too far from here," said Mrs. Drazil.

"Then why'd you say you came from Brazil?" asked Benjamin.

"No, I said I wasn't from Brazil," said Mrs. Drazil.

"Have you ever been to Brazil?" asked Eric Fry.

"No," explained Mrs. Drazil. "It was just a little joke. Brazil rhymes with Drazil. I thought it might help you remember my name."

Terrence laughed. "Drazil—Brazil!" he shouted. "That's funny!"

Several other kids laughed too.

But not Deedee. She had heard of Mrs. Drazil somewhere. She was sure of it. And whatever she had heard, she was sure it wasn't good.

"What's a Brazil?" asked Eric Ovens.

"Brazil is the largest country in South America," said Mrs. Drazil.

"Oh," said Eric Ovens. "I thought it was one of those things that, you know, women wear, you know, on their bosom."

Several kids laughed.

"No, that's a brassiere," said Mrs. Drazil.

There was more laughter.

Stephen was shocked. "She said 'brassiere'!" he whispered. "Right in class!"

"I know, I heard her!" said Jason.

But Deedee still didn't trust her, even if she did say "brassiere" right out loud.

There was a television show that Deedee liked to watch. It was about real criminals. At the end of the show, they always asked the viewers to call the police if they knew where any of the criminals were.

Deedee wondered if she had seen Mrs. Drazil on that show.

"Does anybody have any questions they'd like to ask me?" asked Mrs. Drazil.

Ron raised his hand.

Mrs. Drazil pointed to him.

"How old are you?" asked Ron.

Dana gasped. "You're not supposed to ask someone *that*!" she said.

"Especially someone as old as Mrs. Drazil!" said Mac.

Mrs. Drazil smiled. "I don't mind," she said. "I'm sixty-six years old. You can ask me anything you want."

"Anything?" asked Joy.

"I'm a teacher," said Mrs. Drazil. "That's what I'm here for."

Paul raised his hand. "How much do you weigh?" he asked.

"One hundred and twenty-four pounds," said Mrs. Drazil.

"How much money do you make?" asked Eric Bacon.

"I'm a substitute teacher," explained Mrs. Drazil. "So I only make money on days that I teach. Then I make fifty-one dollars and eighteen cents a day."

"What a rip-off!" said Jenny. "You should make at least two hundred!"

"That would be nice," said Mrs. Drazil. "But I'm a teacher because I love to teach. I love to see young children learn."

Joy raised her hand. "How many men have you kissed in your whole life?"

Mrs. Drazil thought a moment as she appeared to be counting on her fingers. "Thirty-one," she said.

Everyone gasped.

Deedee raised her hand.

Mrs. Drazil smiled at her. "Yes, the girl in the pretty flowered T-shirt."

"Have you ever been in jail?" asked Deedee.

"No," said Mrs. Drazil.

"Are the police after you?"

"No," said Mrs. Drazil.

Deedee still didn't trust her.

"Okay," said Mrs. Drazil. "Before we get started I want to say one more thing. I enjoy teaching so much that sometimes I get a little carried away. I talk too much. So if I start to get boring, will somebody please raise your hand and tell me."

"For real?" asked Todd. "You want us to tell you to stop talking?"

"And we won't get in trouble?" asked Bebe.

"No, of course not," said Mrs. Drazil. "You'll be helping me and the rest of your class. You're not going to learn anything if you're bored."

"Cool!" said Terrence.

"Oh, I suppose when I first started teaching, I used to be a little more strict," said Mrs. Drazil. "I even worried about things like whether my students had clean fingernails or if their shirts were tucked in." She laughed. "But times have changed. I've changed. Besides, the kids were a lot worse back then. At least *some* of them."

For just a second her sweet face turned sour as she looked at her notebook on her desk.

Then she smiled again. "I believe teaching requires mutual cooperation. I will cooperate with you, and you need to cooperate with me. If we work together, we will have a very enjoyable learning experience."

Her face turned sour again. "But if you cross me, you will be very, very sorry." She ran her fingers over her blue notebook. "Oh, maybe not today, maybe not tomorrow, but *someday I will get you!* You can run, but you can't hide."

She smiled. "Okay, let's get started."

14. A Light Bulb,
a Pencil Sharpener,
a Coffeepot,
and a Sack of Potatoes

"Galileo was a great scientist," said Mrs. Drazil. "He was born in Italy in 1564 and died in 1642. He was the first person to use a telescope to study the stars. And he also helped figure out the laws of gravity."

"Oh, I know about gravity," said Joe. "Mrs. Jewls pushed a computer out the window. It fell a lot faster than a pencil."

"I don't think so," said Mrs. Drazil. "Galileo proved that all objects fall at the same speed. He conducted a very famous experiment. He dropped lots of different objects off the Leaning Tower of Pisa. The Leaning Tower of Pisa is in Italy. It was built in—"

Todd raised his hand. "You're getting a little boring," he said.

"Oh, my goodness, am I?" asked Mrs. Drazil.

Rondi, Leslie, Paul, and Calvin nodded their heads.

"I'm sorry," said Mrs. Drazil. She thought a moment. "I know!" she exclaimed. "Let's do the experiment here!"

The children cheered. They loved experiments.

Mrs. Drazil rubbed her hands together. "Let's see. We'll need a coffeepot, a pencil sharpener, a light bulb, and . . ." She thought a moment. "We need something heavy."

"An elephant's heavy," said Benjamin.

"There are no elephants in Wayside School," said Mrs. Drazil.

Everyone laughed.

"How about a sack of potatoes?" asked Ron. "I bet Miss Mush has one."

"Go see," said Mrs. Drazil.

"There's a coffeepot down in the office," said Stephen.

"Go get it," said Mrs. Drazil.

"If I had a screwdriver, I could get the pencil sharpener off the wall," said Eric Fry.

"I've got a screwdriver!" said Jenny.

"Can we use a fluorescent light bulb?" asked Bebe. She looked up at the ceiling.

"I guess so," said Mrs. Drazil.

"How do I get it?" asked Bebe.

"You're the scientist," said Mrs. Drazil. "You figure it out."

Bebe put her chair on top of her desk and stood on it. She still couldn't reach the ceiling. "Hey, Benjamin, let me have your chair!"

She put Benjamin's chair on top of hers, but she still wasn't tall enough.

Calvin dumped the wastepaper basket onto the floor. "Try this," he said.

Bebe turned the trash can upside down and put it on top of Benjamin's chair. Then she climbed on top, but she still couldn't quite reach.

Leslie brought the class dictionary. Jenny and Dana donated their math books. Sharie grabbed Mrs. Drazil's old blue notebook.

"Put that down!" yelled Mrs. Drazil. "Right now!"

Sharie dropped the notebook. Mrs. Drazil's kindly old face had suddenly turned mean.

"Don't ever touch that again!" Mrs. Drazil ordered.

Sharie returned, trembling, to her seat.

Everyone was staring at Mrs. Drazil. She smiled sweetly. "Go back to what you were doing," she said.

Jason threw Bebe his lunch box. She set it on top of the books, then climbed on top. Standing on her tiptoes, she was able to pull the cover off the fluorescent light. She grabbed the light just as the pile collapsed beneath her.

She fell to the ground, triumphantly holding the unbroken light bulb high above her head.

Ron returned with a sack of potatoes from Miss Mush.

Stephen returned with Mr. Kidswatter's coffeepot.

Eric Fry unscrewed the pencil sharpener from the wall.

Mrs. Drazil wrote "Coffeepot," "Sack of Potatoes," "Pencil Sharpener," and "Light Bulb" on the blackboard.

"We're going to drop all four objects out the window at the same time," she said. "How many people think the coffeepot will hit the ground first?"

"Is there coffee in it?" asked John.

"It's about half full," Stephen reported.

Eight kids thought the coffeepot would hit the ground first. Sixteen thought the sack of potatoes would hit the ground first. Three thought the light bulb would be first. Only Terrence thought the pencil sharpener would hit first.

Jason, Jenny, Joe, John, and Joy were the judges. Mrs. Drazil sent them outside.

Stephen held the coffeepot out one window.

Bebe held the light bulb out another.

Eric Fry held the pencil sharpener out another.

And Ron held out the sack of potatoes.

Everyone else crowded around to watch. With everyone on the same side of the classroom, the school leaned a little bit, just like the Leaning Tower of Pisa.

"On your mark. . . . Get set. . . . Let go!" said Mrs. Drazil.

The objects fell through the air and smashed against the pavement.

A short while later, the judges returned. Their clothes were splattered with coffee. Jenny had bits of potatoes in her hair.

"Was the pencil sharpener first?" asked Terrence.

"It happened so fast," said Joe. "They all hit about the same time."

"But the coffeepot made the coolest explosion," said Jason.

"I think the light bulb hit the ground last," said John.

"Well, that's possible," said Mrs. Drazil. "Gravity causes all objects to fall at the same rate. But air slows them down. That's called air resistance. And that's good. Otherwise raindrops would kill us. Air resistance slows all things down a little bit, but it has a greater effect on very light objects, such as a piece of paper. And of course the shape of the paper is important too. A crumpled-up piece of paper will fall faster than—"

"You're getting boring again," said Mac.

Mrs. Drazil stopped talking.

"Now we need a new pencil sharpener," said Leslie.

Paul licked her ear.

15. An Elephant
in Wayside School

The bell rang for recess, and the children exploded out of the building.

Louis, the yard teacher, was ready with a big pile of red and green balls.

The kids called, "Hi, Louis!" and "Over here, Louis!" as he tossed the balls to them: over his shoulder, behind his back, through his legs.

Deedee came charging out of the building. Usually by the time she got to the playground, there were no good balls left, but she could see one red ball by Louis's foot.

She knocked over a kid from the tenth floor and shouted, "Hey, Lou—"

Suddenly she stopped.

She had just remembered where she'd heard of Mrs. Drazil.

It was from Louis! He had once told her about the meanest teacher he'd ever had when he was a kid.

She hurried over to her friends to make sure. "Hey, Todd!" she called.

Todd was playing tetherball with Ron. As he turned to look at Deedee, the ball came around and bonked him on the head.

"Do you remember when Louis told us about the meanest teacher he ever had?" asked Deedee.

Todd shook his head. After being conked by the tetherball, he couldn't remember anything.

"I remember," said Jason, who was in line to play. "Whenever Louis got in trouble, the teacher used to put the wastepaper basket on his head!"

"That's right!" said Jenny. "And then Louis would have to keep it there the rest of the day. And everyone would laugh at him. And then the teacher would call on him to answer questions from the blackboard, but he couldn't see the questions, so she'd give him an F!"

"Do you remember the teacher's name?" asked Deedee.

Her friends shook their heads. Todd couldn't even remember his own name.

"I think it was Mrs. Drazil," said Deedee.

They ran to Louis.

"Hey, Louis!" said Jason. "What was the name of that mean teacher you once had when you were a kid?"

"Which one?" asked Louis.

"The one that put the trash can on your head," said Jenny.

Louis shuddered just thinking about her. "Mrs. Drazil," he whispered.

The kids looked at each other.

"What color hair did she have?" asked Jason.

"Brown," said Louis. "Why?"

"We have a substitute teacher," explained Deedee. "She's real nice."

"Good," said Louis.

"Her name is Mrs. Drazil," said Deedee.

"Whoa, I'm getting out of here," said Louis. He started to run, but the kids grabbed him.

"It's okay," said Jenny. "It can't be the same teacher. *Our* teacher is nice."

"And her hair isn't brown," said Jason. "It's white."

Louis relaxed a little bit.

"You want to come up and meet her?" asked Deedee.

"No way!" said Louis.

"Oh, you're so silly, Louis," said Deedee. "She's not the same teacher. And besides, you're a teacher now too."

"Oh, yeah, I forgot," said Louis.

"C'mon, Louis," said Deedee. She held his hand and led him up the stairs.

They entered the classroom.

Mrs. Drazil was putting some of the children's work on the bulletin board.

"Mrs. Drazil," said Deedee. "We brought our yard teacher up to meet you."

"It's very nice to meet you," said Mrs. Drazil as she pinned up Joe's arithmetic test. "Exercise is so important for young minds and bodies." She turned around.

Louis's face paled. "Well, it was nice to meet you," he said very quickly. "I've gotta go. Bye!"

"Stay right where you are, Louis!" ordered Mrs. Drazil.

He froze.

Mrs. Drazil slowly walked to her desk. She picked up the old blue notebook.

"The notebook!" whispered Louis.

Mrs. Drazil opened it and flipped through the pages. "Here we are," she said. She removed a piece of paper and handed it to Louis. "Is this your homework?" she asked.

Louis looked at it.

"You were supposed to copy it over, weren't you?" asked Mrs. Drazil.

"That was over fifteen years ago," said Louis. "I don't remember."

"I do," said Mrs. Drazil.

"Oh, now I remember!" said Louis. "I was going to copy it over. But then my pencil point broke, so I went to sharpen it, but the pencil sharpener fell on my foot, so I had to go to the hosp—"

"I don't want any of your famous excuses, Louis," said Mrs. Drazil. "I just want the homework. You may share Deedee's desk."

Louis sat next to Deedee.

"And remember, Louis," said Mrs. Drazil. "I know your tricks."

Deedee watched Louis struggle with his homework. "Sorry, Louis," she said.

"Don't be sorry," said Mrs. Drazil. "It's for his own good. And I expect neatness, Louis, or else you'll just have to do it again."

He frowned.

Mrs. Drazil stood over him and watched him work. "Your fingernails are filthy," she said.

"I'm the yard teacher," Louis tried to explain. "I spend a lot of time outside, in the grass and dirt and stuff."

"I don't want excuses," said Mrs. Drazil. "I want clean fingernails. And while you're at it, shave off that mustache. It looks like a hairy caterpillar crawling across your face!"

"Not my mustache," said Louis.

"Unless you want me to rip it off for you," said Mrs. Drazil.

Deedee felt terrible. "I can't believe Mrs. Drazil still remembers you after all this time," she said.

"An elephant never forgets," muttered Louis.

"I heard that," said Mrs. Drazil. She put the wastepaper basket on Louis's head.

16. Mr. Poop

Joy, Maurecia, and Jenny were playing jump rope out on the playground. School hadn't started yet.

Maurecia and Jenny were twirling. Joy sang as she jumped:

> *"My mama wore pajamas to the*
> *grocery store.*
> *She smashed a bunch of eggs on the*
> *grocery floor.*
> *One dozen, two dozen, four dozen, six.*

*She dumped a bunch of jelly jars into
the mix.
Grape jelly, apricot, don't forget
cherry.
Orange marmalade and wild
strawberry.
A man walked by and fell in the glop.
He slid next door to the barber shop.
His icky–sticky body got covered in
hair.
He tore a hole in his under—"*

Joy tripped over the rope. It wasn't her fault.
Maurecia had suddenly stopped twirling.

"Hey!" said Joy. "What's the big idea?"

"Look!" said Maurecia.

A very handsome stranger was walking toward them.

The girls stared at him.

"Good morning, Maurecia," said the stranger.
"Jenny. Joy."

"How do you know my name?" Maurecia
asked nervously. She wasn't supposed to talk to
strangers.

"I've known you a long time," said the stranger. "I see you almost every day."

Maurecia was beginning to feel scared. She

looked around for Louis, the yard teacher, but didn't see him. "I can scream real loud," she warned.

"Oh my gosh!" said Jenny. "It's Louis!"

Maurecia looked at the stranger. He did sort of look like Louis.

Except his hair was combed. His shirt was tucked in. He was wearing a tie. And there was skin between his nose and mouth.

He had shaved off his mustache.

"That's Mr. Louis to you," said Louis. "I'm a teacher, and I expect to be treated with respect."

"You want to play jump rope, uh, Mr. Louis?" asked Maurecia.

Louis was great at jump rope. He could even do it blindfolded. He was the one who taught Joy the song she was singing at the beginning of this story.

"No, thank you, Maurecia," said Louis. "I don't play games. I'm an adult."

"But you're a yard teacher," said Jenny.

"No, I'm a Professional Playground Supervisor," Louis corrected her. He walked away.

"Wow!" whispered Maurecia. "I never knew Louis was so handsome!"

Jenny patted her heart. "I think I'm in love," she said.

"I thought he looked kind of goofy," said Joy.

Up in class, everyone was talking about the new Louis.

"He looks so weird without his mustache," said Calvin.

"He's handsome!" said Bebe.

"He got mad at me for running across the blacktop," complained John. "He made me go all the way back to the edge of the blacktop, then walk across it. And I had to call him Mr. Louis."

"I am very proud of Louis," said Mrs. Drazil. "He has always been a troublemaker. But I think he is trying to be good. We should all give him a chance."

Joy stared at Mrs. Drazil. *It's your fault,* she thought. *You made him shave off his mustache.*

At recess, Louis refused to pass out the balls.

"I haven't washed them yet," he said.

"You're going to wash the balls?" asked Eric Bacon.

"They're filthy," said Louis. "And they all have the wrong amount of air in them."

"I don't care," said Eric Fry.

"I do," said Louis. "Before I can let you play with them, I have to clean them and pump them up with the precise amount of air as specified by POOPS."

"POOPS?" asked Eric Ovens.

"The Professional Organization Of Play-ground Supervisors," explained Louis.

He showed them the POOPS handbook.

"Well, what are we supposed to do?" asked Eric Fry.

"Just play and have fun," said Louis. "But remember, stay off the grass. No running on the blacktop. No eating. And no excessive shouting."

The three Erics walked away. "What a booger brain!" muttered Eric Bacon.

Louis heard him.

"That's Mr. Booger Brain to you, young man," he said.

The next day, when the kids tried to go outside for recess, they only made it down to the fourth floor. The stairs were completely jammed with other kids from lower classrooms.

"Hey, what's going on?" shouted Joy.

"Louis won't let anyone outside," somebody shouted back. "He's painting the blacktop!"

"But I have to go to the bathroom!" yelled Stephen.

"Now he's gone too far!" said Joy. "Excuse me, out of my way, sorry, coming through!" she said as she squeezed in and out of kids, crawled through legs, climbed over heads, until she made her way to the door at the bottom of the stairs.

Louis was slopping black paint across the blacktop. Joy could see him through the glass door. Next to him was a big bucket of paint.

"MR. LOUIS!" she shouted so loud that even the kids back up on the fourth floor had to put their hands over their ears.

He came to the door.

"What are you doing?" Joy demanded.

"The blacktop isn't black," explained Louis. "It's gray. A blacktop is supposed to be black. It's right here on page forty-three of the POOPS handbook."

He opened the book and showed page forty-three to Joy.

Joy grabbed the book and threw it out across the graytop. It landed *plop* in the bucket of black paint.

All the kids behind her cheered.

"You're the Poop!" said Joy.

Louis's red face turned even redder. The place where his mustache used to be turned purple.

"That's Mr. Poop to you," he said.

17. Why the Children Decided They Had to Get Rid of Mrs. Drazil

1. She was nice.

"I made cookies for everyone this morning," Mrs. Drazil announced.

Everyone cheered.

2. She thought up ways to make learning interesting.

"I made five dozen cookies," she said. "There are twelve cookies in a dozen. So, who can tell me how many cookies I made?"

Joe waved his arm back and forth. "I know! I know!" he said.

"Okay, Joe," said Mrs. Drazil. "How many cookies did I make?"

"Five dozen," Joe said proudly.

3. She was patient.

"Yes, I made five dozen cookies," said Mrs. Drazil. "I told you that. But how many cookies are there?"

"Five dozen," said Joe.

"But how many cookies are in five dozen?" asked Mrs. Drazil.

"Huh?" asked Joe.

"How much is twelve times five?" asked Mrs. Drazil.

"Uh, just a second," said Joe. "Can I use pencil and paper?"

"Certainly," said Mrs. Drazil.

Joe took out a piece of paper and a pencil. He wrote the number five on the piece of paper, then tore it into twelve pieces. "Sixty!" he said.

Nobody quite understood Joe's mathematical methods.

4. She was fair.

"Yes, there are sixty cookies," she said. "And there are twenty-eight children in the class. So, how many cookies should each child get?"

Bebe raised her hand. "A hundred," she said.

"You can't have a hundred cookies," said Mrs. Drazil. "I only made sixty."

"Make some more," said Bebe.

"I made sixty," said Mrs. Drazil. "I'm not making any more."

"Okay," Bebe said with a sigh. "I'll take sixty."

"We have to divide them evenly," said Mrs. Drazil. "How many cookies should each child get, so that every child gets the same amount?"

John raised his hand. "Everyone can have two cookies," he said, "and there will be four left over."

"Can I have them?" asked Bebe.

Allison raised her hand. "Everyone can have exactly two and one-seventh cookies," she said.

"Very good, Allison," said Mrs. Drazil. "And John, you were right too." She gave everyone exactly two and one-seventh cookies.

5. She was a good cook.

"Best cookies I ever had in my whole life!" said Stephen.

Everyone agreed.

"I got the recipe from Miss Mush," said Mrs. Drazil.

"You did?" several kids said together.

"I just added a pinch of this and a little of that," said Mrs. Drazil.

6. She knew what a goozack was.

"Jason, would you please open the door?" she said.

Everyone gasped.

"What's the matter?" she asked.

"You said the D-word!" said Dana.

"Door?" asked Mrs. Drazil.

Everyone gasped again.

"You're supposed to call it a goozack," explained Dana.

"Who said so?" asked Mrs. Drazil.

"Mr. Kidswatter," said Dana.

"Mr. Kidswatter is a goozack," said Mrs. Drazil.

Yes, Mrs. Drazil was smart. She was nice. She made learning interesting. She was patient and fair. And she even could make Miss Mush's cookies taste good.

But she made Louis shave off his mustache.

And so she had to go.

18. The Blue Notebook

They had a plan. It all depended on Sharie.

Everyone just hoped she wouldn't fall asleep first. Sharie often fell asleep in class.

C'mon, Sharie, thought Deedee. *You can do it.*

Sharie looked out the window. The sky was full of big, fluffy clouds. She yawned. The clouds looked like giant pillows.

Sharie imagined herself wrapped up in one of those clouds, soft and cozy. She pulled her blue-and-red overcoat snugly over her head.

Her eyes closed. Then they opened wide. "Whazzat?!" she shouted.

"Sharie?" said Mrs. Drazil.

"Look!" shouted Sharie, pointing out the window. "It's a— Hurry!" Her long eyelashes stuck straight out.

Mrs. Drazil hurried to Sharie's desk. "What is it?"

"A spaceship!" said Sharie. "From outer space!"

On the other side of the room, Deedee dropped her pencil. She bent down to pick it up, then stayed down.

Deedee was part of the plan too. She had a dangerous mission. She had volunteered for it. She felt it was her duty, since she was the one who had brought Louis up to meet Mrs. Drazil in the first place.

"You don't have to do it," Ron had told her. "Mrs. Drazil would have seen Louis sooner or later."

"No, I'll do it," Deedee had bravely replied.

Now she crawled across the floor.

Mrs. Drazil looked out the window. "Where?" she asked.

"Wait, it went behind a cloud," said Sharie.

"What did it look like?" asked Mrs. Drazil.

"Like a giant hamburger," said Sharie. "But there was a zizzle stick hanging down from the bottom!"

Deedee crawled to the teacher's desk. She reached up and quietly opened the top drawer. She removed the blue notebook.

Mrs. Drazil stared out the window. "What's a zizzle stick?" she asked.

"I don't know," Sharie said very mysteriously. "They don't have them here on earth."

Deedee crawled safely back to her seat.

At recess everyone crowded around Deedee as she went through the blue notebook.

"Louis once put a frog in Mrs. Drazil's shoe," she said.

"Why wasn't her shoe on her foot?" asked Jenny.

"It doesn't say," said Deedee. "There's a whole list of bad things Louis did. And he made it sound like Mrs. Drazil picked on him for no reason!"

"No wonder she put a trash can on his head!" said Todd.

"What else did he do?" asked Eric Bacon, who was always looking for new ideas.

But Deedee had already turned the page.

"There are other kids a lot worse than Louis," she said, flipping through the pages.

"What are you looking for?" asked Ron.

"I don't know yet," said Deedee. "But I'll know it when I see it."

She saw it!

It was a note to Mrs. Drazil from a girl named Jane Smith. Deedee read it aloud.

Dear Lizard Face,

Guess what? I didn't do my homework again! HA HA HA! And there's nothing you can do about it because you're too stupid and ugly! HA HA HA! My family is moving away tomorrow! And you don't know where! HA HA HA! Rub a monkey's tummy! By the time you get this letter, I'll be gone. Rub a monkey's tummy with your head!

> *Love and Kisses,*
> *Jane Smith*

Everyone was shocked.

"How old is that letter?" asked Myron.

Deedee checked the date, then did the math in her head. "Jane Smith wrote it twenty-six years ago."

"And look," said Ron, reading over Deedee's shoulder. "Jane didn't do her last twelve homework assignments!"

After recess Sharie saw the UFO again, and Deedee returned the notebook to Mrs. Drazil's desk.

Now all they had to do was find Jane Smith.

19. Time Out

Miss Zarves taught the class on the nineteenth story. There is no nineteenth story. And there is no Miss Zarves.

You already know all that.

But how do you explain the cow in her classroom?

Miss Zarves drew a triangle on the blackboard. "A triangle has three sides," she said, then pointed to each side. "One, two, three." She drew a square. "A square has four sides. One, two, three, four."

She walked around the cow to the other side of the board. She drew a pentagon, a hexagon, and a perfect heptagon. "A heptagon has seven sides," she said.

Miss Zarves was very good at drawing shapes. When most people try to draw heptagons, there is always one side that sticks out funny. But Miss Zarves's heptagon was perfect. Every side was the same length, and every angle the same degree.

It was a great talent. But nobody appreciated her.

Nobody appreciated anything she did. It was like they didn't know she was there.

She counted the sides on the heptagon. "One, two, three, fo—"

"MOOOOO," said the cow.

Miss Zarves dropped her chalk. She glared at the cow. "I hate this!" she shouted.

It was a brown cow with a white head.

"It's all right, Miss Zarves," said Virginia, her best student. "I'll get the chalk for you."

"No," said Miss Zarves. "Leave it where it is. The cow made me drop the chalk. The cow should pick it up."

Her students gaped at her.

"I will not continue," said Miss Zarves, "until that cow picks up the piece of chalk and draws an octagon on the board!" She folded her arms across her chest, stared at the cow, and waited.

Ray raised his hand.

"Yes, Ray," said Miss Zarves, arms still folded across her chest.

"Uh, cows can't pick up chalk," said Ray.

Miss Zarves sighed. "I know," she said. "And I can't teach with a cow in my classroom!"

No one had ever seen Miss Zarves so upset. She usually had a pleasant disposition.

"It's okay, Miss Zarves," said Virginia. "I don't mind the cow."

"You get used to it after a while," said Ray.

"What cow?" asked Nick. "Oh, that one! I forgot it was there."

Miss Zarves smiled. She knew her students were trying to make her feel better.

"Other classrooms have goldfish or hamsters," said Virginia. "It's really no different."

"No," said Miss Zarves. "I won't have it! All my life I've tried to be accommodating. I've never been one to complain. And what has it gotten me? A cow!"

She shook her head. "When I was a little girl, my friends never did what *I* wanted to do," she said. "I always had to do whatever *they* wanted to do.

105

"And my teacher never called on me in class. She always called on the kids who just shouted out without raising their hands, even though she said she wouldn't. She'd say, 'I won't call on you if you don't raise your hand,' but then she always did anyway. But I was a good girl. I never shouted out.

"And she always did things alphabetically, so I was always last, if there was time for me at all.

"My parents were too busy for me. They were always dressing up and going out to fancy parties. I had to tuck myself in at night and wish myself sweet dreams."

She took a tissue out of her sleeve and wiped a tear from her eye.

"Still, I always tried to keep a smile on my face. Well, not anymore! The days of walk-all-over-Miss-Zarves are finished!"

She threw open her classroom door. "The squeaky wheel gets the grease!"

"What are you going to do?" asked Virginia.

"I'm going out there!" said Miss Zarves. "And I'm not coming back until I get some grease!"

She stepped outside. She decided she'd go right to the top! So she headed down the stairs—to the principal's office.

Joy and Maurecia were coming up the stairs.

"Todd is uglier than stupid," said Maurecia.

"You're crazy!" said Joy. "He's stupider than ugly."

"Oooh," teased Maurecia. "I'm going to tell Todd you think he's cute."

Miss Zarves stepped in front of them. "What are you children doing out of class?" she asked.

"I didn't say he was cute," said Joy. "He's just not as ugly as he is stupid."

"That means you think he's handsome," said Maurecia. "Are you going to *marry* him?"

"I asked you a question," said Miss Zarves.

"Ugh, gross!" said Joy.

"I'm a teacher," said Miss Zarves. "That means you are supposed to listen to me."

Joy and Maurecia walked right past her.

Miss Zarves sighed, then continued down to Mr. Kidswatter's office. She took a deep breath to steady her nerves. She was about to knock but then changed her mind and just marched right in. "Hey, Kidswatter, I want to talk to you!"

The principal was making a rubber-band ball.

"Do you hear me?" asked Miss Zarves.

He opened his desk drawer and looked for some more rubber bands.

"If you don't answer me right now," said Miss

Zarves, "I'm walking out the door and never coming back!"

Mr. K. pressed the buzzer on his phone. "Miss Night, you need to order more rubber bands."

"That's it!" said Miss Zarves. "I'm leaving. Good-bye. I quit!"

She walked out of the school and took a deep breath of fresh air.

"Please don't go, Miss Zarves," said a voice behind her.

Startled, she turned around.

"We need you," said a bald-headed man. He was standing between two other men. Both had black mustaches, and one carried a black attaché case. The bald man didn't have a mustache.

"Can you see me?" she asked.

"Yes, of course," said the bald man. "And we appreciate all your hard work."

"You do?"

All three nodded very sincerely.

Miss Zarves was touched. "I've been teaching for thirty years," she said. "And nobody has ever said that before."

"Well, it's not easy being a teacher," said the bald man.

"I don't get any respect," said Miss Zarves. "People treat me like I'm a nobody."

"It's not easy being a teacher," said the man with the attaché case. "You have to work long hours for very little money."

"I've never gotten paid," said Miss Zarves. "And this is the first time in thirty years I've ever left the building."

"It's not easy being a teacher," agreed the other man with a mustache.

"Even the book I'm reading to my class," said Miss Zarves. "The author makes fun of teachers!"

"It's a tragedy," said the bald man.

"Then why do it?" asked Miss Zarves. "Why teach anymore? I could quit and nobody would care."

"The children need you," all three men said together.

Miss Zarves sighed. "I like to teach," she said. "I really do. I love the children. It's just—"

She stopped and wiped her eyes.

The man with the attaché case opened it. He took out a handkerchief and handed it to Miss Zarves.

"Thank you," she said, blew her nose, then gave it back to him.

He placed it back in his attaché case.

"Can you at least get the cow out of my classroom?" she asked.

The bald man smiled. "I'll see what I can do," he said.

Miss Zarves smiled as she slowly shook her head. Then she turned and walked back into the building.

20. Elevators

Mr. Kidswatter's voice came over the loudspeaker. **"Good morning, boys and girls!"**

There was the usual pause.

"I have a very important announcement," said Mr. K. **"Elevators have been installed in Wayside School!"**

For a second, the kids on the thirtieth floor were too stunned to speak. Then everyone went crazy!

"Yahooooo!" yelled Sharie.

"Hot diggity dog!" shouted Dameon.

Everyone was yelling and jumping.

"Zippity doo dah!" shouted Mrs. Drazil.

Cheers could be heard coming from every classroom in Wayside School. The higher the classroom, the louder the cheers.

"Now, before you all rush out and use the elevators," said Mr. Kidswatter, "I want to talk a little bit about elevator safety.

"I don't want the same kind of chaos that we have on the stairs every day. I don't know how many times I have to tell you. When you go up the stairs, stay to the right. When you come down the stairs, stay to the left. But still, everyone keeps bumping into each other.

"Well, that won't happen on the elevators. I have personally designed a special safety system.

"There are two elevators. One is blue. One is red. When you want to go up, you take the blue elevator. When you want to go down, you take the red elevator. It's that simple. It can't go wrong! The blue one only goes up. And the red one only goes down.

"By the way, has anyone seen my coffee-pot?"

And so, at last, Wayside School got elevators. A blue one and a red one. They each worked perfectly one time—and never could be used again.

21. Open Wide

The good news: Jason got to leave school early.

The bad news: He had a dentist appointment.

"I'll never ever eat candy again," he promised the Tooth God as he headed down the stairs. "And I'll brush my teeth after every meal. I promise. Even if it's just a snack. I'll bring my toothbrush to school! Just please, *please* don't let her find any cavities."

"I've heard that song before," answered a voice inside his head. "Every time you go to the dentist, it's the same thing. But then, a week later, you're eating candy and forgetting to brush your teeth."

"This time I really, really mean it," Jason promised.

"Too late," said the voice.

An hour later Jason was lying on his back in the dentist chair.

"Open," said the dentist.

His dentist was named Dr. Payne. She had long fingers and even longer fingernails.

Jason opened his big mouth. He had the second biggest mouth in his class.

"Wider," said Dr. Payne.

Jason stretched his mouth until his cheeks hurt.

"That's good," said Dr. Payne. "Now just a little bit wider."

The veins in Jason's neck bulged out as he stretched his mouth even wider. His eyes watered. His throat was dry.

"Okay, just hold it like that," said Dr. Payne. She turned on the sucking machine and put a tube in Jason's mouth.

The machine made a gagging noise as it sucked out his last drop of moisture.

As Dr. Payne poked around at his teeth

she said "Tsk, tsk" and "Oh, my!" several times.

"So how do you like school?" she asked.

"Aghaa," said Jason.

"What grade are you in?"

"Aakhalak," said Jason.

"Well, just remember," said Dr. Payne. "It's very important to always listen to your teachers and do whatever they say."

She poked a tooth with a long, pointed dentist tool.

"AAAAHhhhhhhhh!" Jason screamed in agony.

"Did that hurt?" asked Dr. Payne.

Jason shook his head. If he told her it hurt, she might think it was a cavity. If she couldn't find it herself, he certainly wasn't going to tell her about it.

"Are you sure?" asked Dr. Payne. She poked the same spot.

This time Jason didn't make a sound. Tears and sweat dripped down his face.

The receptionist came into the room.

"Yes?" said Dr. Payne.

Jason was glad for the break.

"Kendall's mother is on the phone," said the receptionist. "She refuses to pay her bill."

"What?!" exclaimed Dr. Payne. "How dare—"

"She says you pulled the wrong tooth."

"Give me the phone!" shouted Dr. Payne.

The receptionist handed it to her.

"This is Dr. Payne. What do you mean you're not paying your bill? . . . Well, then, just bring Kendall back in here, and I'll pull that one too. I'll pull them all! But you still have to pay me.

"Your lawyer! I don't care what your lawyer said. You can tell your lawyer to rub a monkey's tummy! . . . You heard me! Rub a monkey's tummy with your head!"

She slammed down the phone.

Jason looked at the diploma hanging on the wall. Before his dentist got married, her name was Jane Smith.

His big mouth opened wider.

22. Jane Smith

"I found Jane Smith," Jason told Stephen the next morning when he got to school.

"You better tell Deedee," said Stephen.

They hurried across the playground.

A whistle blew. "No running!" ordered Mr. Louis, the Professional Playground Supervisor. "Now I want both of you to go back to the edge of the blacktop, and *walk* this time."

The boys went back the way they came, then came back the way they went.

Deedee was sitting on a bench. She had been benched by Mr. Louis for excessive noisemaking.

"I found Jane Smith," Jason whispered as he walked past her. . . .

. . . Deedee and Jason entered the classroom together. Mrs. Drazil was seated behind her desk. As they passed in front of her, Deedee stopped and said, "Did you have a nice time at the dentist yesterday, Jason?"

"Yes, Deedee," said Jason. "It was very nice."

"I wonder if we have the same dentist," said Deedee. "What is your dentist's name?"

"Her name is Dr. Payne," said Jason. "But that hasn't always been her name."

"It hasn't?" asked Deedee.

"Oh, no," said Jason. "Before she was married, her name was Jane Smith."

"Jane Smith?" asked Deedee. "Is that spelled J-A-N-E S-M-I-T-H?"

"Yes, that's how you spell Jane Smith," said Jason. "But like I said, that's not her name anymore. Her name is Dr. Payne. She works at the dentist office at 124 Garden Street."

They took their seats. . . .

* * *

. . . Late that afternoon Dr. Payne finished work and walked out of her office. It had been a good day. She had drilled twenty-five teeth.

She made sixty dollars for every tooth she drilled. Twenty-five times sixty dollars is $1,500. Not bad for a day's work.

Of course, not all the teeth really had cavities, but how would any of her patients find out?

She got into her fancy silver-and-black sports car and drove away. She sang along with the radio.

She didn't even notice the old beat-up green station wagon in her rearview mirror.

She lived in a mansion next to the lake. There was a stone wall around the house. She pressed a button in her car, and an iron gate opened. The gate closed behind her as she headed up the long and winding driveway.

A moment later the old green station wagon stopped and parked next to the gate. A woman got out, walked around to the back, and opened the tailgate. She pulled out a ladder. She set the ladder up against the wall.

Under her arm she carried an old blue notebook. . . .

. . . Dr. Payne's butler handed her a drink. The cook was making dinner.

Dr. Payne's dog, cat, and husband were wait-

119

ing for her in the den. Her dog's name was Brussels, and her cat's name was Sprouts. She petted them both.

Her husband's name was Sham. She petted him too.

"Hi, darling, how was your day?" he asked.

"I made fifteen hundred dollars," said Jane.

They hugged and kissed. They loved each other, but they loved money even more.

Then they had dinner by candlelight as they watched the sun set over the lake. After dinner they sat out on the deck, under the stars.

Sprouts lay purring on Jane's lap. Brussels sat faithfully by her side.

Life was perfect.

"I love you, darling," she said, petting Sprouts.

"And I love you," said Sham.

"I was talking to the cat," said Jane.

The butler stepped out onto the deck. "Excuse me, madam," he said, "but there's an elderly woman out in the yard."

Jane's long fingernails dug into her cat's neck.

"I wonder how she got past the gate," said Sham.

"I don't know, sir," said the butler. "She's probably hungry. Perhaps I can give her some leftover—"

"No!" shouted Jane. "Get rid of her!"

"Let me have a look," said Sham. He followed the butler back into the house.

He returned a moment later. "Darling, you'll never guess who's here. One of your former teachers! Isn't that just the sweetest—"

Jane screamed. She jumped to her feet. Sprouts flew off her lap and into the hot tub.

"What's wrong?" asked Sham.

"You idiot!" shouted Jane. "I told you to get rid of her!" She kicked her dog out of the way, then climbed over the railing and jumped off the deck to the ground, fifteen feet below.

Mrs. Drazil came out onto the deck. "You can't get away from me, young lady!" she hollered.

Jane hurt her ankle pretty badly when she hit the ground. It was either sprained or broken. She lay on the ground in agony as she looked up at her former teacher.

"You have homework to do," said Mrs. Drazil, looking down at her.

Jane's face twisted with pain. "Rub a monkey's tummy!" she shouted, then struggled to her feet.

She had a suitcase stashed in the boathouse, just in case this ever happened. She hobbled to it, grabbed it, then limped down to the lake, dragging her suitcase behind her.

Mrs. Drazil hurried down the steps on the side of the deck.

Jane groaned as she threw her suitcase into a motorboat. Then she pulled herself aboard and started the engine.

"Darling, come back!" Sham shouted from the deck as he watched the boat sputter across the water.

Mrs. Drazil climbed into an old rowboat. "I'll find you, Jane Smith!" she shouted into the darkness. "You can run, but you can't hide!"

Jane's voice echoed back across the black water. "Rub a monkeeee's . . . tumm-mmy . . . with . . . yourrr . . . heaaaaaaaaaa . . ."

And neither of them was ever seen again.

23. Ears

Wendy had three. Ears, I mean.

She had one ear on each side of her head, just like most people. But she also had a third ear, which lay flat on top of her head.

You couldn't see it. It was completely covered by her thick, frizzy brown hair.

She was an intelligent and lovely young woman. She was gentle and kind.

At least, she used to be. Then she met Xavier and became evil and wicked, but I'll get to that later.

She lived in a small apartment in the big city. She always kept fresh flowers in the vase on her kitchen table.

She didn't have any friends. She was afraid someone might find out about her ear. She was very embarrassed by it.

The one on top of her head, I mean. The other two ears were pretty, as ears go.

Actually, the third ear wasn't ugly. In fact, it looked just like her other two.

It was quantity, not quality, that bothered her.

Then she met Xavier.

It was at a museum. They happened to be standing next to each other looking at the same painting. The *Mona Lisa.*

A guard stood by to make sure they didn't touch it.

Xavier was very handsome. But he was frightfully shy. He was afraid of women.

"That's a beautiful painting, isn't it?" said Wendy.

Xavier blushed. He wanted to speak, but his mouth locked shut with fear. It took all his courage just to nod his head.

But Wendy knew he liked her.

Because there was something else about her ear I haven't told you yet. The one on top of her head, I mean.

It didn't hear normal sounds. It heard people's brains.

Wendy was able to listen to Xavier's secret thoughts. And this is what she heard.

Yes, the painting is very beautiful. But you are more beautiful than the Mona Lisa. *I wish somebody would paint your picture. I would buy it and look at it all day. Alas, if only I had the courage to talk to you.*

Wendy didn't usually listen to other people's thoughts. She thought it was rude, even though the other people didn't know she was listening.

Besides, most people's thoughts were usually boring.

Xavier was getting too nervous standing next to her. He moved on to another painting.

Wendy followed him.

She listened to the lonely man's thoughts. They weren't boring at all. Most of his thoughts were about her, but she also learned a few other things. He liked to read. His favorite author was Charles Dickens. He loved animals, especially dogs.

"That painting reminds me of a book," said Wendy. "*A Tale of Two Cities*, by Charles Dickens. Have you read it?"

"Yes!" Xavier blurted, a little too loudly. "It's my favorite book! I've read everything Dickens has written. Twice. My favorite part is when—"

He suddenly stopped, very embarrassed.

"Please go on," said Wendy.

"No, I don't want to bother you," said Xavier.

"You're not bothering me," said Wendy. "Charles Dickens is my favorite author. I sometimes read aloud to my dog."

"You have a dog?" asked Xavier.

Wendy nodded.

Xavier stared into her dark eyes. "I love dogs," he said, as his brain said, *I love you.*

Wendy and Xavier spent the afternoon together. He could hardly stop talking.

It was like a genie had escaped from a bottle. All the love and emotion that had been buried for so long inside him came pouring out on Wendy.

"I don't even know your name," he suddenly blurted.

"Wendy Nogard," said Wendy.

"I'm Xavier Dalton," said Xavier.

They shook hands and made plans to meet again at the museum the following week.

On her way home, Wendy stopped by the library and checked out *A Tale of Two Cities.* Then she went to the pet store and bought a dog.

A month later Xavier asked her to marry him.

Wendy didn't know what to say. She loved Xavier. And she knew he loved her. But she still hadn't told him about her ear.

The one on top of her head, I mean.

He knew about the other two. He had nibbled on each of them.

"Marriage is a big step," she said. "I'm afraid we haven't known each other long enough."

"I've known you long enough to know I could never be happy without you," said Xavier. "Before I met you, Wendy, I was sad and lonely. But I was used to it. Now I can't imagine living like that again. I don't know what I'd do without you."

He stroked her hair.

"Well, there's one little thing you don't know about me," said Wendy.

His hand bumped into it. "What's this thing?" he asked.

"That's what I was going to tell you about, dear," said Wendy.

Xavier parted Wendy's hair and looked at it. "It's an ear!" he exclaimed.

"Yes, it is," said Wendy. "Some people have two ears. I have three. Now that you know, if you still want to marry me, my answer is yes! Yes, sweetheart, yes!"

"I love you," said Xavier. "That's all that matters to me."

That was what he said. But this is what he was thinking.

127

Oh, gross! You're disgusting! I never want to touch you again! I can't even stand to look at you! You tricked me, you freak! You monster!

And of course Wendy heard every word.

He stood up. "I'll be right back, sweetheart. I bought you diamond earrings as an engagement present. I just need to run back to the jewelry store and buy one more." He hurried out the door.

She never saw him again.

I'm sorry to say this story has a sad ending.

Xavier, thanks to Wendy, got over his shyness. He went out with lots of women but broke each one's heart. He could never love any of them.

There was a hole in his heart. He was in love with Wendy Nogard, but he didn't know it. And so he could never be happy.

Wendy became a bitter and evil person. She was unhappy, and she wanted everyone else to be unhappy too.

Whenever she heard someone thinking happy thoughts, she would listen closely and then do and say just the right thing to make the person feel rotten.

She hated children the most. Every time she passed a playground, she heard them laughing and having fun.

So she became a substitute teacher.

24. Glum and Blah

Miss Nogard entered the classroom on the thirtieth story. She looked at all the bright and chipper faces. She knew by the end of the day they would no longer be bright and chipper.

They would be glum and blah.

She smiled at the class. "Good morning, everybody," she said. "My name is Miss Nogard."

She listened to their brains.

Calvin had spilled orange juice on his lap during breakfast and worried that someone might think he had gone to the bathroom in his pants.

Dana had gotten her hair cut yesterday, and she thought it was too short. She was afraid it made her look like a boy. She was especially sensitive to this because Dana was sometimes a boy's name.

Jason was mad at his older brother, Justin. Justin was in high school. Justin always got good grades and was a star in everything he did. Compared to Justin, Jason felt like a loser. "What's so great about high school?" he had asked this morning. "My school is higher than yours!"

D.J. had heard a song on the radio on his way to school. He hated the song! But it kept playing over and over again in his head.

Bebe had an itch on her leg.

Miss Nogard smiled. The bad stuff always rose to the top of the brain.

Even if a person was very excited about something wonderful, the person still worried about what could go wrong.

Jenny was going horseback riding after school, if it didn't rain. She had never gone horseback riding before. She hoped she wouldn't fall off the horse.

Miss Nogard clapped her hands. "So, who would like to tell me what you've been working on?" she asked.

A few hands went up in the air.

"Oooh! Oooh!" said Mac.

"How about the boy in the orange and purple shirt?" said Miss Nogard.

Everyone looked around.

"The handsome young man sitting right there," said Miss Nogard.

Dana looked at her shirt. It was orange and purple. She pointed at herself and mouthed the word *me*?

"Yes, you," said Miss Nogard.

Dana's face turned red-hot. "I'm a girl," she said.

Everyone laughed.

"Oh, I am so embarrassed!" said Miss Nogard, with her hand over her heart.

"It's not your fault," said Dana. "It's my stupid haircut. I hate it!"

"Oh, no," said Miss Nogard. "You look adorable. I see now you're a very pretty girl."

"I'm ugly," muttered Dana. She buried her head under her arms.

"I'd better call on someone else," said Miss Nogard.

Suddenly, out of nowhere, a brain screamed, *Don't call on me! Whatever you do, please don't call on me!*

It came from Benjamin Nushmutt.

"How about you?" said Miss Nogard, looking right at him.

Just don't ask me my name, thought Benjamin. *I never can say my name in front of people.* He took a breath to steady himself. "Well, we've been reading—"

"First tell me your name," Miss Nogard said sweetly.

The muscles in Benjamin's face tightened. He concentrated real hard, then said, "Benjamin Nushmutt."

"I beg your pardon?" said Miss Nogard.

"Benjamin Nushmutt," he repeated.

"Henderson Schmidt?" asked Miss Nogard.

Benjamin sighed. "Ben-ja-min Nush! Mutt!" he shouted.

"I'm sorry," said Miss Nogard. "I must have been distracted. What did you say?"

Benjamin pressed his lips together. He tried to speak, but his mouth wouldn't open.

"His name is Benjamin," said Jason. "Benjamin Nushmutt."

"Thank you," said Miss Nogard. "That's a very nice name, Benjamin. You shouldn't be ashamed of it."

Benjamin covered his red face with his hands.

She turned to Jason. "You look familiar. Do I know you?"

"I don't think so," said Jason.

She stared at him, as if she were trying to remember. "You're Justin, right?"

"I'm Jason. Justin's my older brother."

"So you're Justin's baby brother!" said Miss Nogard.

Everybody laughed.

"I remember Justin. I substituted for his class once. He was the brightest student I ever taught. You must feel very lucky to have such an exceptional brother."

His feet stink, thought Jason.

For the rest of the day, Miss Nogard kept accidentally-on-purpose calling Jason "Justin."

One by one, she made every child in the class feel miserable. She called Calvin to her desk and asked in a whisper if he had to use the restroom. Whenever she passed D.J., she hummed the song stuck in his head. Whenever Bebe finally stopped thinking about her itch, Miss Nogard would walk by and scratch her own leg.

"It looks like it might rain," she said as she stared out the window at the bright blue sky.

Darn, I'll never get to go horseback riding! thought Jenny.

"I have a nephew who went horseback riding on a day like this," said Miss Nogard. "There wasn't a cloud in the sky. Then suddenly, out of nowhere, it started thundering and lightning. It spooked the horse terribly."

"What happened to your nephew?" asked Jenny.

"Oh, he's fine," said Miss Nogard. "He just broke both his arms and legs. He'll be in a cast for a year. But he has a very positive attitude; that's the important thing. Remember, always keep a positive attitude."

By the end of the day, nobody had a positive attitude. The whole class was glum and blah.

The children walked out of the school building, heads down. Except Jenny, who looked up at the sky, worrying about the weather, although she didn't know if she was more worried about rain or sunshine.

Even D.J. was frowning.

"What's the matter?" asked Louis, the yard teacher.

"Nothing," muttered D.J. "I guess I just had a bad day."

"Don't you like your new teacher?" asked Louis.

"She's real nice," said Dana. *It's not her fault I'm the ugliest girl in the world!*

134

"I like her a lot," said Jason. *It's my brother I hate.*

"Me too," said Benjamin. *I hate myself!*

Louis rubbed his upper lip. His mustache was beginning to grow back. "What's her name?" he asked.

"Miss Nogard," said Bebe as she scratched the back of her leg raw.

"Are you sure?" asked Louis.

"Huh?" asked Bebe.

"I mean," said Louis, "are you sure it's *Miss* Nogard? Not *Mrs.* Nogard?"

"I think," said Bebe. "Why?"

Louis just shrugged.

25. Guilty

Some of the children were working in their workbooks. Others were reading in their readers. And still others were computing on the computer.

Miss Nogard looked from one to another. *Eenie . . . meenie . . . minie . . . Maurecia!* she thought.

Maurecia was stamping a stamp.

"Maurecia," said Miss Nogard. "Will you come here, please?"

Maurecia walked to the front of the room. "Yes?" she said cheerfully.

"Don't 'yes' me, young lady," said Miss Nogard. "You know what you did."

Maurecia looked back at her teacher. *What did I do?* she wondered.

Miss Nogard waited patiently. Everyone was guilty of something.

I didn't do anything, did I? thought Maurecia. *I've been good, I think. Unless she found out about that dictionary page I accidentally tore. No, she couldn't know about that! It happened before she even got here. And I don't think anybody saw me do it.*

"I didn't do anything," she said. *I probably should have told Mrs. Jewls about it,* she realized, *but it wasn't even my fault! I was looking up how to spell 'journey' for my journal, and the page just ripped all by itself.*

"It is one thing to do something wrong, Maurecia," said Miss Nogard. "But when you do, you should admit to it. We all make mistakes. But when you lie about it, you make matters much worse for yourself."

Maurecia nodded as she tried to figure out what to do. If Miss Nogard knew she tore the dictionary page, then of course she should admit to

137

it. But there was no way Miss Nogard could know! It was impossible.

"I don't know what you mean," she said innocently. "I didn't do anything wrong." She smiled at her teacher.

Miss Nogard stared at her a long moment, then said, "Will you please bring me the dictionary?"

The smile dropped off Maurecia's face and crashed on the floor.

The dictionary lay on top of the bookcase. Maurecia numbly went after it. *How could she know?* she wondered. *It's impossible! Maybe she just wants to look up a word.*

She carried the heavy book back to Miss Nogard.

"Thank you, Maurecia," said Miss Nogard, flipping through the pages. "I need to look up 'journey.' "

Maurecia couldn't take it any longer. "I ripped it!" she cried out. "I tore the dictionary. I'm sorry. I don't even know how it happened. I was just turning the page, really! Maybe pages only have a certain amount of turns in them. Like, nine hundred and ninety-nine. Then when you turn the page for the thousandth time, it will rip, no matter who turns it."

Miss Nogard sadly shook her head. "I am very disappointed in you," she said. "Not only did you vandalize the dictionary. But then you lied about it. I thought I could trust you, Maurecia. I guess I was wrong."

"I'm a horrible person," Maurecia agreed. "I'm sorry."

"Don't apologize to me," said Miss Nogard. "It's not my dictionary. It belongs to the class."

Maurecia had to stand in front of the class and tell them she was sorry. Then, since nobody would ever be able to use that page again, she had to read it aloud to the class.

She struggled through the difficult words like "journalism" and "judicious."

"Speak up," Miss Nogard had to keep reminding her. "And everyone needs to pay close attention because there will be a test on it when Maurecia is finished."

"Hey, that's not fair!" complained Jason. "We didn't rip the dictionary. Why should we be punished?"

"It's not punishment," said Miss Nogard. "It is for your own good. Since you can no longer use that page, you need to memorize it."

"Thanks a lot, Maurecia!" griped Jenny.

When Maurecia finished reading it, Miss Nogard made her turn the page over and read the back side of it too.

"But I only ripped the front," said Maurecia. "Not the back."

She finished, then returned to her seat, angry and upset. She wasn't angry at Miss Nogard. Miss Nogard was just being fair, she thought.

But there was only one way Miss Nogard could have known about the torn page, she realized. Somebody in the class must have seen her tear it and then tattled on her.

She looked around the room, from Deedee to Todd to Terrence to Joy. She didn't trust any of them.

One of her friends was a no-good-dirty-double-crossing-snake-in-the-grass!

26. Never Laugh at a Shoelace

"This is a shoelace," said Mac.

Everybody laughed.

Mac was standing at the front of the room, holding his shoelace in his hand. He felt like a fool.

"What a fool!" said Allison.

It all started a minute earlier, when Miss Nogard asked, "Who has something to share for show-and-tell?"

But first you should know something about Mac.

Mac's favorite subject in the whole world was show-and-tell. He loved it. Especially when he was the one doing the showing and telling.

He often looked through garbage cans on his way to school, in search of stuff to show and tell about. Once he found a real gushy love letter. It was covered with something that looked like peach slime. But that wasn't what made it gushy. The gushy part was what was written in the letter. Mac read it to the class with lots of feeling.

So when Miss Nogard said, "Who has something to share for show-and-tell?" Mac reacted without thinking. His arm shot up like a rocket as he almost jumped out of his seat. "Ooooh! Ooooh!" he groaned.

Then he remembered something. *I didn't bring anything for show-and-tell!*

Miss Nogard heard him. Before he could lower his hand, she called on him.

And that was how he ended up with his shoelace dangling from his hand like a dead worm.

"It came from my sneaker," he said. He took off his sneaker and held it up too, next to his shoelace. "See, you stick the laces through the little holes, here. Then tie it in a bow. That keeps it from falling off your foot."

"Duh!" said Dana.

"We know what a shoelace is," said Paul.

"I've been tying my shoes since I was two years old," said Joe.

Calvin and Bebe booed.

"Sit down," said Jason. "You're boring."

The kids in Mrs. Jewls's class never used to be so mean, but they'd been getting grumpier and grumpier ever since Miss Nogard took over.

"Put your shoe back on!" said Maurecia. "Your foot stinks."

Mac felt terrible.

Miss Nogard smiled. "Go on, Mac," she said. "We're all very interested to hear what you have to say."

He tried to think of some way to make a shoelace interesting. "Uh, shoelaces are real important," he said. "There was once this guy. He was a real fast runner. His name was Howard. Howard Speed! He was the fastest runner in the world! But this was back before shoelaces were invented. And so, every time Howard raced, he ran right out of his shoes!"

Nobody seemed very impressed. But then Rondi asked, "Did it hurt his feet?"

Mac shrugged. "I guess," he said.

"I once stubbed my toe on a rock," said Stephen. "It hurt."

"Yeah, and you didn't run as fast as Howard Speed!" said Mac. "He ran so fast that if he kicked a rock, he would break his toe!"

"Did he have blisters?" asked Todd.

Mac smiled. "Man, he had the biggest blisters you ever saw in your whole life! Bleeding blisters!"

"Ooooh," Joe and John said together.

"With pus oozing out!" said Mac.

"Oh, gross!" said Dana, wide-eyed.

Everyone was paying close attention to Mac now.

"Wherever Howard went," said Mac, "he left a trail of bloody footprints."

"Cool!" said Terrence.

"And so they had to invent something to keep Howard's sneakers on his feet," said Mac. "First they just tried nailing his shoes to his feet."

"Yowza!" Bebe exclaimed.

"Why didn't he just use Velcro?" asked Jason.

"Howard lived in Africa," explained Mac. "Velcro trees only grow in Australia. So then they tried gluing his shoes to his feet. And that seemed to work. But then, whenever he took off his shoes, like to take a bath or something, he'd peel off a layer of skin."

"Yuck-ola!" shrieked Allison.

"But finally Thomas Edison invented the shoelace, and Howard never ran out of his shoes again."

"Did he win all his races after that?" asked John.

"Well," said Mac, "the next race was for the championship of the whole world. Howard got off to a real fast start. It looked like he would win for sure. But shoelaces were still a new invention, and Howard wasn't quite used to them yet. Right before he reached the finish line, his shoelace came untied. He tripped over it and fell flat on his face. He broke his nose, lost all his teeth, and had two black eyes!"

"Wow," said all three Erics together.

"So remember," said Mac, as he held his shoelace high in the air. "Never laugh at a shoelace!"

Everyone applauded.

27. Way-High-Up Ball

Eric Fry, Eric Bacon, and Eric Ovens were playing way-high-up ball. They had made up the game themselves.

All you needed were two things—a pink rubber ball, about the size of a tennis ball, and a real tall school.

Eric Ovens threw the ball way high up. It bounced off the school, just above the third-story window.

"Three-pointer," called Eric Bacon.

They shoved and elbowed each other out of the way as they waited for it to come down. At the last second, Eric Fry jumped and caught it.

He got three points. Eric Ovens also got three points since he was the thrower.

Eric Fry threw the ball way high up. It bounced off a window on the fifth floor.

"Five-pointer!" called Eric Ovens.

All three Erics jumped for it. It bounced off their fingertips and hit the ground.

The teacher on the fifth story stuck her head out the window. "Hey, what's going on down there?" she shouted.

The three Erics looked away and whistled.

There's one more thing about way-high-up ball I haven't told you. You're not allowed to play it. The Erics had already broken one window.

Eric Bacon looked up, surprised. "Are you talking to us?" he asked.

"Something just banged against my window," said the teacher.

"Was it a bird?" asked Eric Ovens.

The teacher stared at the children a moment longer. Then she pulled her head inside.

Eric Fry threw the ball way high up. It was a six-pointer!

All three fought for position as they waited for

it to come down, but at the last second, a hairy arm reached above them and caught it.

The arm belonged to Louis, the yard teacher.

"Can I play?" asked Louis. His mustache had grown back completely.

"Sure!" all three Erics said together.

"What do I have to do?" asked Louis.

"Just see how high up against the school you can throw it," said Eric Fry.

Louis gripped the ball tightly in his hand. He reached way back, then let it fly.

"Wowww!" the three Erics said together as they watched the ball soar up in the air.

It hit up above the eighth-story window; then Louis caught his own rebound.

"Sixteen points!" said Eric Bacon.

"Throw it again, Louis," said Eric Ovens.

Now that Louis was playing, lots of kids from all over the playground came to play too.

Louis threw the ball way high up. It hit above the eleventh story, then bounced back over everyone's head.

There was a mad scramble for the ball. Bebe finally came up with it.

"Give it to Louis," said Eric Ovens.

"No, let Bebe throw it," said Louis, who always tried to be fair.

Bebe threw a two-pointer.

Jason caught the rebound. "You want to throw it, Louis?" he asked.

"No, you go ahead," said Louis.

Jason threw a glopper.

A glopper is when the ball goes straight up in the air and comes down without touching the building.

Eric Bacon caught it. "Here, Louis," he said.

"No, you throw it," said Louis.

"But you can throw it so much higher," said Eric B.

"We want to see how high you can throw it, Louis," said Leslie.

"C'mon, Louis!" everyone urged.

Louis shook his head. "The game is for you kids, not for me."

"Miss Nogard is watching," said Bebe slyly.

Louis glanced at Miss Nogard, who was standing just outside the front door. "Give me the ball," he said.

The kids cheered.

Louis reached way down, almost to the ground, then hurled it up with all his might.

The ball reached the fifteenth floor, halfway up the school!

"Wow!" everyone said together.

"I got it," called Terrence as he circled under the ball, waiting for it to come down. His knees wobbled.

The ball bounced off his face. "Cool," he said as blood flowed out of his nose.

"That was a world's record, Louis!" exclaimed Eric Ovens.

Louis smiled proudly. He turned to look at Miss Nogard, but she had already gone inside.

"You like Miss Nogard, don't you?" asked Bebe.

"She seems like a nice person," said Louis.

"She's pretty too," said Eric Bacon as he nudged Louis in the side.

"Well, she is kind of cute," Louis admitted.

"Oooooh," said Joy.

"But do you *love* her?" asked Jenny.

Everyone giggled. Louis's red face got even redder.

"You should ask her out on a date," said Eric Fry.

"No, I don't think that's a very good idea," said Louis.

"Why not?" asked Eric Ovens. "I think you two would make a real cute couple."

"Bring her flowers," said Dana.

"Buy her candy," said Maurecia.

"Tell her she's got eyes like the moon," said Bebe.

"Eyes like the moon?" asked Louis.

"Girls love it when you tell them that," said Bebe.

"Forget that gushy stuff," said Eric Bacon. "Just walk right up to her and say, 'Hey, baby! How about a date?'"

"Just like that?" asked Louis.

"This is what you do," said Terrence. "You take her to a real scary movie. And then at the scary part, you put your arm around her."

"Ooooh," said Dana and Jenny.

"No, take her dancing," said Myron. "And hold her real close."

"Ooooooh," said the three Erics.

Louis laughed. "You kids are crazy," he said.

"You're scared of her, aren't you?" asked Eric Bacon.

"You shouldn't be scared," said Eric Ovens. "You're bigger and stronger and faster than anyone on the playground."

"And you've got the best mustache too," said Eric Fry.

"I'm not afraid of her," Louis tried to explain. "It's just—" He looked up at the very tall school. "Miss Nogard is way-high-up there, and I'm way-

151

down-low here. You'll understand someday when you're older."

He picked up the ball and threw it way high up. It hit somewhere between the eighteenth and twentieth story.

And never came down.

There was no nineteenth story.

28. Flowers
for a Very Special Person

Of course Miss Nogard knew all about Louis. The children's brains were buzzing about him.

Louis likes Miss Nogard, thought Stephen.

Louis is in love with Miss Nogard, thought Todd.

Louis wants to marry Miss Nogard, thought Sharie.

But even if she couldn't listen to their brains, she would have found out anyway. "Louis, the yard teacher, is madly in love with you," said Jenny.

"Oh, really?" said Miss Nogard.

"He dreams about you every night," said Calvin.

"He thinks your eyes are like the moon," said Bebe.

Miss Nogard smiled.

"Do you like him?" asked Jenny.

"He's kind of cute," said Miss Nogard.

"Ooooh," Bebe and Calvin said together.

"What about his mustache?" asked Jenny. "Do you like his mustache?"

Miss Nogard thought a moment. "It would probably tickle if he kissed me."

The children gasped as their mouths fell open.

They returned to their desks and told everyone around them what Miss Nogard said.

Miss Nogard smiled. She wondered just how she'd break Louis's heart.

Ever since Xavier broke her heart, she'd become an expert at breaking other people's. She listened to men's brains and knew just what to say to make them fall in love with her.

And then she knew just the right thing to say, at just the right moment, to shatter their hearts into a million pieces. Even the biggest and strongest man would cry like a baby.

She was incapable of love. Her heart was clogged with bitterness and hate. And besides, she knew no one would ever love someone with three ears.

For just a second she felt a pang of sadness. Because she really did think Louis was kind of cute. Like a puppy dog.

She could almost feel the tickle of his mustache.

"Miss Nogard thinks you're cute," Jenny told Louis at recess.

"She's hot for you, Louis!" said Mac.

"She wants to kiss you!" said Bebe.

"C'mon, let's play kickball," said Louis.

They played kickball, but it was weird. Louis, who was probably the best kickball player ever, did terribly. He tripped over the ball when he tried to kick it. And when Terrence kicked a pop-up, Louis tried to catch it, but the ball bounced off his head.

"What's wrong with Louis?" asked Ron. "Is he sick or something?"

"Yes," said Jenny. "He's got a real bad disease. And it's spelled L-O-V-E."

The next morning Louis came to school with a bunch of flowers in his hand.

Jenny saw him. "Are those for Miss Nogard?" she asked.

"Oh, I don't know," said Louis. "I passed a field of wildflowers on the way to school. I thought I might give them to someone special." He winked at her.

He headed toward the school building. Jenny followed.

"*Oooh,* flowers!" said Bebe.

"Are you going to give them to Miss Nogard?" asked Calvin.

"Oh, I don't know," said Louis. "I think she might have a pretty face, I mean vase."

Calvin and Bebe followed along with Jenny.

Louis entered the building.

Miss Nogard was in the office. She was getting her mail from her box. Her back was to him.

Louis froze.

"Go on, Louis," urged Jenny.

But Louis just stood there. The flowers rattled in his shaky hand, and several petals fell to the floor.

Mr. Kidswatter came out of his office. "Good morning, Louis," he said. "What have you got there?"

"Uh, these are for you," said Louis. He thrust the flowers into Mr. Kidswatter's hand.

"They're lovely!" said Mr. Kidswatter.

Miss Nogard turned around. "Those are very pretty, Mr. Kidswatter," she said, then headed up the stairs.

Louis watched her go.

"No one's ever brought me flowers before," said Mr. Kidswatter. "You may not believe this, Louis, but I don't have many friends." He put his hand on Louis's shoulder. "You're like a son to me," he said.

"And you're a maggot-infested string bean," muttered Louis.

"What?" asked Mr. K.

"I said, you're a magnificent human being."

29. Stupid

"Did anyone have any trouble with the homework?" asked Miss Nogard.

They all shook their heads.

Ron shook his head too. *Homework?* he thought. *What homework?*

"Good," said Miss Nogard. "Well, in that case, there won't be any homework tonight."

Everyone cheered.

"Let's just quickly go over the answers," she said. "Ron, what was your answer to question one?"

Ron's stomach flipped over. He fumbled with his notebook. "Uh, just a second," he said.

"That's okay, we'll wait," said Miss Nogard.

Ron flipped through the pages. "What question are we on?" he asked.

"Question one," said Miss Nogard.

"Um, I couldn't get that one," said Ron.

"Oh," said Miss Nogard. "Well, that's okay, Ron. As long as you tried. Who knows the answer to question one?"

A handful of hands went up in the air.

Seven lima beans, thought Jason.

Seven lima beans, thought Rondi.

Six cucumbers, thought Deedee.

Seven lima beans, thought Stephen.

Miss Nogard called on Deedee.

"Six cucumbers," Deedee said proudly.

"No, I'm sorry," said Miss Nogard. "The answer was seven lima beans."

Ooh, I had that! thought Jason.

She should have called on me! thought Rondi.

Deedee is stupid, thought Stephen.

"Okay, question two," said Miss Nogard. "Ron, did you get that one?"

Ron squirmed in his seat. He flipped through his papers. "What question are we on?" he asked.

"Question two," said Miss Nogard.

"Uh, I couldn't get that one either," said Ron.

Miss Nogard looked at him a moment. "Okay, who knows the answer to question two?"

Abraham Lincoln's hat, thought Todd.

Abraham Lincoln's hat, thought Joy.

Abraham Lincoln's hat, thought Bebe.

George Washington's left shoe, thought Calvin.

"Yes, Calvin," said Miss Nogard.

"George Washington's left shoe!" said Calvin.

"No, I'm sorry," said Miss Nogard. "The answer was Abraham Lincoln's hat."

I knew it! thought Todd.

Calvin's stupid, thought Joy.

"Ron, did you get the answer to number three?" asked Miss Nogard.

Ron shook his sorry little head. He wished he had just told her the truth, but now it was too late.

"Anyone?" asked Miss Nogard.

Chairs and bears, thought Benjamin.

Coats and goats, thought D.J.

Chairs and bears, thought Mac.

Chairs and bears, thought Deedee.

Miss Nogard called on D.J.

"Coats and goats?" he said hopefully.

"No, chairs and bears," said Miss Nogard.

What an idiot! thought Benjamin.

"Question four," said Miss Nogard. "Ron?"

. . . And so it went. Miss Nogard went through

the entire homework assignment, and nobody gave a correct answer.

"I'm very disappointed," she said when they were finished. "You obviously didn't understand it. So I'm afraid I'm going to have to assign homework tonight after all."

Everyone groaned.

"I don't like it any better than you do," said Miss Nogard. "But it's for your own good."

She assigned three pages of homework, plus they had to do yesterday's homework over again as well.

But nobody blamed Miss Nogard. They liked her! She didn't even want to give homework.

They blamed each other.

It's not fair! thought Benjamin. *I only missed one problem. But I have to do extra homework because everyone else is so stupid!*

It was the same all around the room. Nobody missed more than two problems. Everyone thought everyone else was stupid!

Miss Nogard smiled as she listened to their thoughts.

I hate Joe! thought John.

I hate Calvin! thought Bebe.

I hate Joy! thought Maurecia.

I hate Allison! thought Rondi.

And everyone hated Ron.

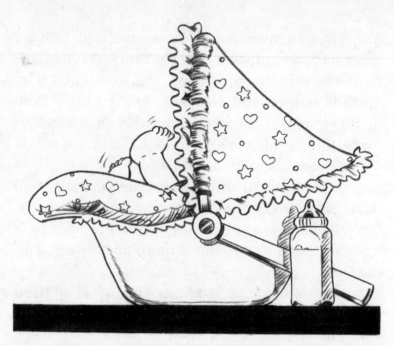

30. The Little Stranger

Wayside School was no fun anymore.

"Hey, out of my way, buster!" said Deedee as she pushed past Ron on her way to her seat.

"Hey, keep your hairy paws to yourself!" said Ron.

Nobody had any friends. Everybody hated everybody—except Miss Nogard. They all liked her.

But then a miracle happened.

A new kid came to school.

The new kid couldn't talk. She had no teeth. She was almost bald.

She was beautiful.

Her name was Mavis Jewls. She was only four days old.

She really was a new kid.

Mrs. Jewls carried her into the classroom.

And when the baby came through the door, all the hate flew out the window.

Louis came in behind them carrying a bassinet, a diaper bag, an assortment of toys, and a baby bottle.

"It's Mrs. Jewls and her baby!" Todd exclaimed.

Louis set the bassinet on Todd's desk. Mrs. Jewls gently laid her baby down in it, on soft yellow blankets.

Everyone crowded around the little stranger.

"Look at her totally tiny toes!" Bebe squealed. "Aren't those the cutest things you've ever seen in your whole life?"

"Check out her nose!" said Myron.

"Oh, she's so beautiful, Mrs. Jewls," said Joy. "Can I touch her?"

"Sure," said Mrs. Jewls.

They took turns touching the baby.

"Goo-goo, goo-goo," said Mac as he gently shook Mavis's little hand.

"Iggle wiggle poo poo," said Allison, tapping her on the nose.

"Iggle wiggle poo poo poo," said Rondi, tickling her foot.

"Yibble bibble," said Todd.

"Ooh goo boo boo," cooed Joe.

"She's never going to learn to talk around you kids," said Mrs. Jewls with a laugh.

Dana was so happy she cried. She hugged Mrs. Jewls.

They all took turns hugging Mrs. Jewls.

Of course, there was one person who wasn't happy. "May I hold her, Mrs. Jewls?" Miss Nogard asked sweetly.

Mrs. Jewls looked at the substitute teacher.

"It's okay," said Allison. "Miss Nogard's a real nice teacher."

"Sure, go ahead," said Mrs. Jewls. "I'm sorry for interrupting your class like this."

"Oh, that's quite all right," said Miss Nogard, picking up Mrs. Jewls's baby. "She's just adorable."

The window by Sharie's desk was wide open. *That's kind of dangerous*, Miss Nogard realized. *Somebody might accidentally drop something out the window.*

She slowly moved toward it as she swayed with the baby. "I've heard so much about you, Mrs. Jewls," she said. "The children have missed you."

"I've missed them too," said Mrs. Jewls.

There was a rubber-band ball on the floor next to Sharie's desk. Sharie had been making it, although it wasn't nearly as big as the one Mr. Kidswatter had been making.

If I tripped over that rubber-band ball, something awful might happen, thought Miss Nogard.

She was just about to step on it, when suddenly she became very curious about the kind of thoughts babies had. She had never listened to a baby's brain before.

Miss Nogard held Mavis close to her heart and listened. . . .

She gasped. Her face turned white, and her legs wobbled beneath her. As she tried to get her balance, she stepped on the rubber-band ball and fell toward the open window.

Louis jumped over Sharie's desk and grabbed her just in time.

Mrs. Jewls hurried over.

Miss Nogard tenderly handed Mrs. Jewls her baby. Then she fainted in Louis's arms.

It is impossible to describe, in words, exactly what Miss Nogard heard when she listened to Mavis's brain.

Babies don't think in words.

Miss Nogard heard pure love. And trust. And faith. With no words to get in the way.

It was a love so strong that it dissolved away all the bitterness that had been caked around her heart.

She opened her eyes.

"Are you all right, Miss Nogard?" asked Stephen.

All the children were very worried about her.

Miss Nogard smiled at Louis, who was still holding her. "I'm fine," she said, then took a couple of steps to steady herself. "In fact, I think I'm better than I've been in a long time." She laughed, then hugged Stephen.

"You should feel very proud of your class," she told Mrs. Jewls. "They are bright, well behaved, and just a pleasure to teach."

"We are?" asked Maurecia.

Miss Nogard fluffed Maurecia's hair. "Yes, you are," she said.

Maurecia smiled up at her.

"I know," said Mrs. Jewls. "As I told my obstetrician—"

"Your what?" asked Joy.

"Obstetrician," said Mrs. Jewls. "That's the doctor who helped me have my baby. Then, once a baby is born, she gets a new doctor. That doctor is called a pediatrician. That's different from a podi-atrist, who is a doctor who takes care of people's feet. There are many different kinds of doctors. There's also a—"

Todd raised his hand. "Mrs. Jewls, you're starting to get a little boring," he said.

Mrs. Jewls made Todd write his name on the blackboard under the word DISCIPLINE.

"Hey, Louis!" shouted Mac. "Ask Miss Nogard out on a date!"

Everyone looked at Louis.

Miss Nogard looked at him too.

"Do it, Louis!" said Leslie.

"I really would like to get to know you better, Miss Nogard," he said.

"Ooooh," said Paul and Leslie.

"Way to go, Louis!" cheered D.J.

"Call me Wendy," said Wendy Nogard.

"Ooooh," said Bebe and Calvin.

"Okay, Wendy," said Louis. "And you can call me Louis."

"I already do," said Wendy. She smiled at him.

He smiled back. "So what do you say?" he asked. "Would you like to go out sometime?"

Miss Nogard hesitated.

"Say yes, Miss Nogard!" urged Jenny.

Miss Nogard took a deep breath. "I like you,

167

Louis," she said. "But I think there is something you should know about me first."

She bent over and parted the hair on top of her head.

Everyone crowded around as they tried to get a good look.

"It's an ear!" shouted Jason.

"Yes, it is an ear," said Miss Nogard.

"Cool!" said Terrence.

"Can I touch it?" asked Dana.

Everyone took turns touching her ear.

The one on top of her head, I mean.

"So, Louis, are you sure you still want to go out with me?" she asked.

Louis held her hands in his. "I like you a lot," he said. "It doesn't matter how many ears you have." He paused for a second. "How many ears do you have?"

"Just three," she assured him.

"I think your ears are beautiful," said Louis. "I think your nose and eyebrows are beautiful."

Miss Nogard didn't have to read Louis's mind to know he was telling the truth. She could see it in his eyes.

His eyes were like the moon.

She kissed him. His mustache tickled.

Everybody oooohed.